Tank

PRAISE FOR THE WORKS OF M. MALONE

"I am now officially in love with the Alexander family."
--Smitten by Reading (Grade: A-) on One More Day

"Malone has a winner with The Alexanders series! Please keep them coming!"
--Joyfully Reviewed on One More Day

"Nicholas is perfect leading man material..."
-- 4 stars, Romance Junkies on The Things I Do for You

"Malone gives her reader a story full of smart dialogue, compelling characters, and a strong story-line. The Alexanders and their friends will draw you in and keep you coming back for more."
-- 4 stars, Romantic Reads on He's the Man

This book has angst, humor, sexy times, and love. What more could you ask for? I hope there are going to be more in this series and you can bet I will be first in line.
-- 4 1/2 stars, S.W. & More Book Reviews on He's the Man

I traveled through this book feeling a gamut of emotions: hurt, embarrassment, despair, anger, love, joy, and happiness. In the end, I loved the story and would recommend this book to anyone looking for a happily ever after ending jam-packed with lots of steamy love and intrigue
-- 4 stars, Twin Sisters Rockin' Reviews on All I Need is You

Titles by M. Malone

BLUE-COLLAR BILLIONAIRES

Available Now

TANK
FINN

Future Books

GABE
ZACK
LUKE

THE ALEXANDERS

Available Now

One More Day
The Things I Do for You
He's the Man
All I Need is You

Future Books

Say You Will
Just One Thing

Tank

BLUE-COLLAR BILLIONAIRES #1

M. Malone

Previously published in ALPHAS AFTER DARK

Editor: Daisycakes Creative Services
Proofreader: Leah Guinan

CrushStar Romance
An Imprint of CrushStar Multimedia LLC

For information address CrushStar Romance, 2885 Sanford Ave SW #16301, Grandville, MI 49418

ISBN-10: 1-938789-19-9
ISBN-13: 978-1-938789-19-9

Tank

Chapter One

Tank

Darkness hasn't always been my friend. There was a time when I would have been at home asleep in my bed in the middle of the night. Instead I'm prowling the streets, restless and edgy, looking for an outlet for the anger roiling inside.

I glance to my left and right. I'm standing in an alcove that's slightly hidden off the street. It's easier this way. People tend to get nervous if I just hang out. No one stares outright. But there's always a tell. A glance. A step to the side when we pass so our bodies don't touch. Everyone has a "look" about them and mine apparently says *trained killer*.

A group of people spill out of the bar across the street, music and the sound of their voices carrying to where I stand in the shadows. This part of Virginia Beach is a mecca for local college kids looking to blow off steam on the weekends so I rarely have to go looking for trouble.

Trouble usually finds me.

I see the girl first. She has taken her shoes off and is walking barefoot on the concrete. She's beautiful and dressed to score in a short black minidress that shows off long, tanned legs. It doesn't take long for one of the guys in front of the bar to break off from his friends and follow her. I push away from the wall and follow them at a discreet distance. He hooks an arm around her neck. She looks up at him in confusion but grins blearily. He smiles back, with an expression like he just hit the lottery. My blood pressure spikes a notch.

Oh yes. Trouble you miserable bastard, you always find me.

I step out into the road to cross to their side of the street, pulling the hood of my jacket up and over my face.

A horn blares and a taxi screeches to a halt a few inches from me. The driver's side door opens and the cabbie steps out. "What the hell! Look where you're going!"

I glance at him and then back to the couple. Oblivious, they turn down a side street and out of sight. If I wait any longer, I'll lose them. I haven't slept in forty-eight hours and if I don't make sure the girl is all right, then I won't be able to sleep again tonight. Knowing, seeing, is the only thing that gives me some peace. I run across the street, leaving the cab driver gesturing and cursing behind me. By the time I turn the corner, the street is dark. Empty. Then I hear it.

Crying.

He has the girl pressed up against the wall behind a dumpster. She's struggling, pushing at his shoulders while he's working the dress up her legs. He has his other hand over her mouth. Her stiletto shoes are a few feet away from me, abandoned.

That's all it takes for my veins to turn to ice. This is what happens to me right *before*. It's like a red haze that settles over me, blanketing me with the righteous fury necessary to do what needs to be done.

I don't speak; I just yank the guy off her. The first blow stuns him and all the color drains from his face as he doubles over clutching his gut. My mom's words from earlier today ricochet through my mind, shredding my sanity as surely as bullets.

The cancer's back, Tank.

He raises his arm to protect his face or maybe to strike back; I don't know. I hit him with a rib shot, plowing my fists into him over and over. With every connection, I feel stronger.

I need surgery and I don't have the money.

After a while, I don't hear anything. I don't see anything. There's just me, some random dirtbag in an alley and the sensation of fists hitting flesh. All I can do is feel. Hatred. Power.

Purpose.

A whimper pulls me from my adrenaline frenzy. The girl is slumped against the wall, one hand on the grimy stone behind her as she watches me with horror in her eyes. Slowly, I remember where I am. My breath puffs in front of my face, a cloud of white in the frigid night air. The guy is slumped on the ground, his face a bruised, pulpy mass.

I hold out a hand to help her up and she cringes back. My knuckles are scraped and bruised and my hands are covered in blood. I look like something from a horror movie. I put my hands down and move back so she's not crowded.

"It's okay. He can't hurt you anymore."

She nods but continues to regard me with wide, watchful eyes. I'm not sure who she's more afraid of, me or the would-be-rapist bleeding next to the dumpster.

Even more, I'm not sure I want to know.

"Go. Get out of here."

She stumbles to her feet and leans down to grab her shoes. Then she turns back. "What about you? Are you okay?"

"Don't worry about me." She doesn't move, just stands staring at me, her gaze dropping to my bloody hands, so I yell, "Get the hell out of here!"

She runs off this time and doesn't look back. I'm glad because there's nothing she can do for me. I'm beyond saving.

Then I turn back to the man slumped on the ground. "But the rest of you aren't."

* * * * *

By the time I make it back to my car, I can already hear sirens in the distance. The girl probably called the police. They usually do. I've learned not to hang around any longer than necessary. A siren screams past just as I'm driving away.

It takes me about ten minutes to get home. There's an open space right next to my motorcycle so I park and cut the engine. My breath forms white clouds in front of my face. Still I don't move to get out yet. Once I'm inside, I'll be alone with my thoughts again. So I sit in my car in the empty, dark parking lot, trying not to think about anything. Finally I push the door open and get out.

There's no one to greet me when I enter my apartment. I live alone. No pets and I don't even have any plants that need to be watered. That's always been the way I liked it but things look different lately. My eyes fall on the letter on the counter. It's still in the same place I left it before I went out tonight. I pick it up and read it again. It's another letter from my father's law firm. Another appeal for me to meet his terms. Another offer of money.

My life is a perfect storm lately, a confluence of every thing I fear the most all happening at once.

Two months ago my mom found out that her cancer is back but she just got around to telling me about it today. She told me that she needs surgery. Some rare, expensive surgery that insurance wouldn't cover even if she'd had it. If that wasn't bad enough, there's the sudden reappearance of the father I haven't seen since I was eight. He's supposedly seen the light and wants to establish a relationship with me and my younger brother, Finn. We were both offered huge sums of money if we agree to meet with him regularly. As long as the visits continue, the money will keep coming.

I turned down the first two offers immediately. But now I have a reason to negotiate. The money could help my mom so that's reason enough to consider it. I work for a private security company and my boss has crazy connections. He recommended a lawyer so I've been meeting with him once a week. He's trying to negotiate terms I can live with.

The terms I really want are for him to go back to whatever cave he's been hiding in for the past twenty years. I don't want to see him at all but for my mom, I'm willing to try. There's not much else I can do for her now. I'm helpless and I hate that feeling.

I drop the letter. There's a rust-colored smudge where my finger touched the white stationery. Blood. I hold up my hands, inspecting the damage. I cleaned the worst of it off with a wet wipe in my car but my hands are still filthy. I walk into my room and strip, dropping everything into a pile in the corner. I walk into the bathroom and turn on the water.

I step into the shower. Water rushes over me and then swirls in a dirty red-tinged pool around my feet. Thoughts of what I'm washing off threaten so I grab the bar of soap on the ledge and rub it all over.

The air in the bathroom is cold, sending a chill over my skin. I wrap the towel around my waist and then rub my hair with another one. I'm clean finally. Although I know the feeling won't last. I can wash the outside but there's nothing I can do for how I feel on the inside.

Some stains are permanent.

At least tomorrow I get to see her again. Everyone hates Mondays but lately they're all that's getting me through each week. Sleep, then I can see her. I comfort myself with the thought.

Tomorrow. Just get to tomorrow.

Emma

I race around my room trying to figure out what I'm going to wear. I'm never a fashion plate but especially when I haven't done laundry. The only clean clothes appear to be the ones I wear to wait tables at my second job. Nothing I wear there is appropriate for daylight hours. I toss aside a miniskirt and a glittery top. I need to find something respectable to wear in the next five minutes.

Rummaging through my closet produces a black skirt that's only marginally creased and a striped button down shirt that I never wear because it's too tight. A glance in the mirror on the back of the closet door proves what I already suspect to be true. I look like I've been digging around in trash bins for discarded clothes.

People are going to put change into my coffee cup if I go out looking like this.

I open the door and collide with my sister, Ivy. "Morning. Can I borrow something to wear?"

She eyes my striped shirt and then nods her head. "If that's your alternative, then yes. Hold on."

I follow her to her room but she holds up a hand. "Wait. I'm not alone. Jon stayed the night."

Great. It's a struggle to keep the annoyance off my face. Jon is a lawyer. We met him when he came to the law office where Ivy and I work on behalf of his client, Mr. Marshall.

How did I not hear them come in last night? I must have been dead to the world. Working two jobs has finally caught up with me. But if I'd known that he would be here, I would have gotten up early and left before now. Tired is better than annoyed and disgusted. I can't say any of this to Ivy so I just settle for "Okay."

The door to her room opens and Jon steps into the hall. His dark hair is rumpled and he's got about three days' worth of stubble going on. Ivy gazes up at him and if this were a cartoon, I'm sure there would be little animated stars dancing in her eyes.

"Morning baby." She leans up to give him a kiss. He returns the caress, one hand snaking down to curve around her waist. As he does it, he holds my gaze the entire time.

I contemplate barfing right then and there.

"Never mind. I'll just wear this. You're still covering for me this morning right? I have my financial aid meeting at school."

Ivy gives an exaggerated sigh. "I'll be there. Calm down. I sincerely doubt Patrick cares who is up front answering phones as long as someone is there to do it."

Ivy and I both work for Patrick Stevens, an old friend of the family. I work the front desk while she helps him part-time with bookkeeping and other administrative tasks. After our parents died, he was the one who helped us settle the estate. I'm not sure what we would have done without his help.

Actually I do know. We probably would have lost the house. After all the creditors were tallied and the life insurance was paid, there was nothing left. We were lucky to be able to stay in the house we grew up in at all.

I don't agree with her assumption that he won't care who's up front but I don't have time to argue. The finance office at the local college only accepts appointments at certain times. A year ago, I was in school studying biology. I was planning to go to veterinary school after I finished my undergraduate degree. After our parents were killed, I was too unfocused to continue. Tears still threaten when I think about that day. I blow out a breath and push the ugly memories away.

I had to drop out but I'm finally ready to go back. I've been waiting for weeks to find out whether I've been approved for financial aid for the next school year. I can't miss this meeting.

"Great. Thanks. I'll come straight there when I'm done. I wanted to go check on Mr. Marshall but it can wait."

She makes a face. "Better you than me. I don't have the patience to sit around talking about nothing. That's all old people want to do. I don't know how you do it."

"Maybe she's hoping to be wife number five." Jon smirks when he sees my confused look. "Hell, you're not much younger than the last one."

I have to physically hold myself back from rolling my eyes. He is so sleazy. It's a mystery to me how that sweet old man deals with Jon's slick persona. Then again, he must be used to dealing with arrogant spoiled men.

My face heats thinking about Tank Marshall. He is exactly the kind of guy that I've always avoided. Tall and muscled with the smug aloofness of the naturally beautiful. He's got that same "I'm the center of the universe" arrogance going on that Jon does. It's a shame that one of the first men I feel raw physical chemistry with is exactly the kind of guy I need to stay far away from. I've seen violence, real violence, before so there is nothing about a *bad boy* that I find appealing.

Ivy claps her hands. "It's gross but that would be awesome. Marry the billionaire Em and all our problems are over."

"It's not like that between us. He's a nice old man. We're friends." Not that Ivy would understand the idea of being friends with a man. Sometimes I think my sister only sees two things when she looks at a guy: his dick and his wallet. Friendship is a foreign concept.

She scoffs. "Only you would consider an old geezer your BFF."

I tuck my shirt into my skirt and hustle into the kitchen. I need coffee and something to eat. I have two pieces of bread in the toaster and the coffee percolating when Jon appears in the doorway to the kitchen. I suppress a groan. I see him at work and now he's invading my home.

It feels like I can't escape him sometimes.

"Why didn't you tell me you needed money for school, Emma?

I'm sure we can work something out." His eyes roam over my bare legs. It disgusts me that he does this, sometimes right in front of Ivy.

The thing is, he's not even attracted to me.

My sister is *gorgeous*. She's got dark wavy hair and big dramatic brown eyes. I have wispy blond hair and plain gray eyes. She's all smoldering screen siren while I look like the plain country mouse next to her. He's not hitting on me because he's overcome with lust. He's doing it because he's a pig. I've tried to tell Ivy but she doesn't want to hear it. She thinks that he's just flirtatious and doesn't mean anything by it. Love is blind and all that, I guess.

"I've got some loans lined up. I'll be fine."

He leans against the counter and I have to stop so I don't bump into him. He's wearing pajama bottoms but no shirt. If I want my coffee, he's going to make me press up against him to get it.

Not happening.

"Forget it. I'll get coffee on the way." I grab my bag and run out of the house. Ivy calls out to me as the door closes but I don't turn around. There's only so much you can do when someone doesn't want to see the truth.

* * * * *

I smooth my black skirt over my knees and try not to fidget. Across the desk, Mr. Christopher Higgans holds my academic future in his hands. He's been working with me for the past few months to make sure that I can start school again in the fall with a full schedule. I've been applying for every grant that I can for the following school year so that I can finish my bachelor's degree. Loans are always available but I don't want to graduate with a huge cloud of debt hanging over me. I'm hoping that I'm eligible for some scholarships or something.

"Miss Shaw, I've been over your application. There are quite a few loans that we can set up for you. Also you qualify for the Pell Grant."

I lean forward to review the documents he's pushed across the desk toward me. The numbers are far lower than what I was hoping for.

"So, this is all I can get?"

"This is a great package. The Pell Grant doesn't have to be repaid."

"But the rest of it does? That's a lot of debt."

I'll only be able to take a full semester of classes if I stop working at the law office. My parents left money for me to use for college but I've worked so hard not to touch it. But if I go to school full-time, even with the loans, I'll need to use some of that money to live on. I had considered taking some weekend classes but if I can only do one or two classes a semester, it'll take me forever to finish. I really hate the idea of touching my emergency fund. Once it's gone, I'll have nothing to fall back on.

"Well, yes. But student loans are deferred. You don't have to repay them until you're finished with school. You should be able to start next year with a full semester of classes. And don't forget that you applied for a few grants that will be awarded soon. The committees will notify you directly if you are selected." He's smiling broadly so I can't do anything except smile back and shake his hand before I leave.

The campus of Southern Virginia Community College is a nice place for a walk on a crisp spring day. My sweater doesn't provide much protection from the biting wind but the sun is warm on my face and the breeze is fresh. My parents were so proud that Ivy and I both went to college. My mom finished her degree but my father was a metalworker at the shipyard.

He'd been obsessed with the idea of his daughters getting a college education and I don't think he took a deep breath until the day I moved into the dorms here. Due to Ivy's wild behavior in high school, I think both my parents considered it a minor miracle that neither of their daughters ended up addicted to anything or pregnant before graduation.

Would he have done things differently if he'd known what was coming for him, I wonder? The thought of *that day* hits me in the chest and I halt right in the middle of the pavilion. Instantly I'm back there, in my room, my mom pushing me into the closet and telling me to call for help.

I suck in several deep breaths, feeling lost in the middle of the students who pass me talking excitedly about classes, friends and what they did over the weekend. They pass me by and have no idea that I'm stuck in my personal hell. With the sounds of gunshots ringing in my ears and my mother's screams outside the door.

My bag falls off my shoulder and I let it drop to the ground. I learned how to control the panic attacks in therapy. I focus on the rhythm of my breath, the beat of my heart and the ground below me. I breathe in and hold it for a count of three, then let it out. The artificial breathing pattern slows the rate of my heart and the sense of panic recedes a little. Finally I look around, suddenly aware that I'm standing in the middle of the courtyard gasping for breath.

I pick up my backpack and force myself to start walking. I'm just starting to get my life back on track so I can't allow myself to go back there. Maybe I'm being foolish to think that I'm ready to come back but it's a fallacy that I need to get me through each day. Next year, I'll be in class all day and doing homework all night. I'll need to be focused.

That day has already stolen everything from me. If let it, it'll steal any hope I have for the future. I can't allow that to happen. I don't want to look back on my life and think of all the things I didn't do and never had. That's why I'm so determined to go back and finish my degree. One and a half semesters and I'll be done with my undergraduate degree. Then I can apply to veterinary school. Now all I need to do is figure out where to get the money for all this schooling.

I tilt my face up into the wind and make a promise. *Almost there, Dad.* I'll get back here and finish what I started.

No matter what I have to do.

Chapter Two

Tank

She's not here.

I'm in my lawyer's office for the third time this month, squashed into a hard wooden chair that's too small for my six foot five inch frame. It still feels weird to say that, *my lawyer*, like I'm some kind of big shot now or something. But it's true. I have a lawyer and an accountant.

I also have a huge stack of money sitting in a trust with my name on it.

Shifting as much as I can in the narrow seat, I lean back and avert my gaze from the brunette currently sitting behind the secretary's desk. She's beautiful but she's not *her*. She looks like she'll faint if our eyes meet one more time, although to be fair I have been glaring at her for the past ten minutes. There's not much else in the room to look at.

There's an older woman with a cane and a small white dog in her purse that yaps every time someone enters or leaves the room. A middle-aged man in the corner mumbles under his breath while working on a crossword puzzle. A guy in a suit sits a few feet away typing into a laptop.

Waiting rooms are not my favorite places. No matter how hard they try to be comfortable, they never get it quite right. Inevitably they are either too cold or too warm. The piped in music is too loud or it's eerily silent. Everyone is staring at everyone else and pretending not to. Since I'm usually the biggest one in the room, you guessed it. Most of the attention is directed at me.

There's only one reason I've been voluntarily coming here for the past few weeks to sit in uncomfortable chairs all while paying for the privilege.

To see *her.* The one person that makes all the noise in my head subside.

And now she's not even here.

The outer office door bursts open and a gust of cold air sweeps through the room, stirring the little dog into a yapping frenzy.

"I'm sorry. Sorry." A young woman rushes past, a flurry of blond hair and apologies, and places her bag on the floor behind the secretary's desk. I sit up straight, watching. The brunette smiles at her with genuine affection. They whisper back and forth before the other woman gets up and walks down the hallway leading to the offices.

The blonde glances over at me before tucking a few of the stray hairs around her face behind her ears. It takes her a few minutes to get settled. She moves a few things around on the desk and then pulls a bottle of water from her oversized bag. She's doing an admirable job of appearing busy and engrossed in whatever's on her computer screen but a few minutes later, she looks at me again.

Usually this kind of thing annoys the hell out of me, but for some reason, with her, I don't mind. Maybe it's the madcap cloud of blond hair or the big, wounded gray eyes. I'm not sure what it is, but there's something about this girl. Something that keeps me coming back week after week. I think it's because she never smiles.

"Don't worry I'm still here."

She lets out a surprisingly crude snort. "Like I could miss you. And I wasn't looking for you."

"Okay, okay." I lean back and make a show of spreading my arms over the backs of the chairs next to me. I'm a big dude and I have a wingspan like a giant. Her eyes follow the movement but when she sees me watching, she turns up her nose a little and goes back to her typing.

I chuckle a little. She doesn't like me much and for some reason, it amuses me. I stare at her openly because I know when she notices she'll do that little huffing sound again. She's a pretty little thing. Elegant. The kind of girl who clutches her pearls when I get too close. The nameplate on her desk reads *Emma Lynn Shaw*. Even her name is prissy as hell.

Despite that, there's something about her that I find compelling.

The phone on her desk rings and she answers, her voice a soft whisper in the quiet room. She nods and then places the phone carefully back on the hook.

"Tanner Marshall?" She calls out, looking around at the other people in the waiting room.

The little dog gives an irritated yip. No one else even looks up. Finally her gaze lands on me. I stand and walk over to her, stopping right in front of her desk. It amuses me that she pretends not to know my name. I've been here every Monday for the last five weeks. Surely she knows who I am by now. She also knows that I hate to be called by my legal name. I've told her to call me Tank every time. I've also asked her to dinner every time.

Then again, she looks like the kind of girl who wouldn't remember a guy like me.

"Is he ready for me?"

"Yes. Just go straight through."

Instead of walking down the hallway, I lean against the wall next to her desk. "So, I have to eat dinner again tonight. Just like last week. And the week before that. It's a pesky recurring event, this dinner thing. I'm assuming you're familiar with it?"

"I am aware of it, yes. Sometimes I go wild and have dessert, too. But you know what I like the best?" She leans closer like she's imparting a secret. "Eating it alone."

I wink at her. "One of these days you're going to realize how much you're missing out on."

"One of these days. Not today."

"Ouch. You're brutal for such a tiny thing." But I've achieved my objective. She's almost smiling.

"Mr. Stevens is waiting for you." She gestures toward the hallway again. Her eyes are gleaming as she turns back to her computer. She types a few words and then looks up at me from the corner of her eye.

"Thank you, Emma." I use her name deliberately just to see her blush again. Patrick's office is the first door on the hallway.

When I push it open, he looks up. "Come on in, Tank. Have a seat."

I wave away his offer. "Look, I don't want to waste your time. You can just tell me. Did he agree?"

Patrick looks slightly uncomfortable and I can tell what's happened. "He didn't, did he? Then there's no point in wasting any more time."

"I didn't meet with your father. He sent his right hand man. Mr. Jonathan Boyd."

This news doesn't surprise me. "He couldn't even be bothered to deal with it himself? I'm sure he outsources everything. He probably has someone to wipe his ass when he needs it, too."

Patrick sighs. "I understand that your father isn't … well." He rifles through the stack of papers on his desk. "All these meetings haven't been entirely unproductive, however. I've gathered quite a bit of information that we didn't have before."

He looks up at me. I cross my arms but I don't leave. He's got me interested and he knows it. "What do you mean?"

"Your father's estate is larger than I was originally led to believe."

"He gave me and Finn both half a million dollars each. He's rich. I got it."

Patrick clears his throat. "From what I gather, the amounts he's given you so far are merely a trifle. Since I know your mother needs surgery, I was able to negotiate a higher initial payment as a measure of good faith. It should be wired into your trust fund by the end of the business day. But speaking from experience, money doesn't go very far when you don't have insurance. This money could be the difference in getting competent care for your mom. It's in your best interest to meet his terms. All he's asked for are weekly meetings, an hour each time. Every week you show up, he'll put money in your trust fund. You have very little to lose and everything to gain."

"So, what you're saying is, I have no choice. If I want money to help my mom, then I have no choice." Helpless rage boils inside me. I feel like I'm being slowly railroaded into this, like all my options are being taken away from me by life and circumstance.

"No, you always have a choice. You can walk away. But just be aware of what you're walking away from. This is a lot of money and from what I understand, your father is very ill. He doesn't have a lot of time left."

"Look, I'm not completely heartless all right, but I haven't seen the bastard in almost twenty years. He left us high and dry and he's been off gallivanting around Europe ever since. This money would have been nice when we were growing up and Mom was working her ass off trying to keep us fed."

"I understand that, Mr. Marshall. However, your father wasn't playing around that whole time. He was making his fortune in coal and steel and investing in green energy solutions. His lawyer indicated that if you should agree to meet with him, then the money you'll inherit will be ...substantial."

"I don't want anything from him. He wasn't there for us in life and I don't want shit from him now that he's on his deathbed and feeling guilty."

“Well, the money he's wiring into your account is another five hundred thousand. That money comes with no strings attached. If you agree to his terms, you’ll receive even more. Congratulations, Mr. Marshall. You just became a millionaire."

"What the hell?" I put out a hand and use the wall to steady myself. I'm not sure what I'm supposed to feel. Grateful? Instead I just feel vaguely dirty.

Patrick hands me a folder. The first page has been flipped up to reveal a new letter from my father's law firm.

“Mr. Boyd has asked if I can help notifying the others. Your brother Finnigan was the only one who responded. You wouldn’t happen to know where they are, would you?”

Others? I have no idea what he's talking about and it obviously shows on my face because Patrick points to the list at the bottom of the page. "Your father has plans to split his empire equally amongst his sons."

"I only have *one* brother. Finn."

Patrick looks stunned for a moment. Then he yanks out the chair in front of his desk.

"Perhaps you'd best take that seat now, Mr. Marshall."

* * * * *

My head is reeling by the time I leave the lawyer's office. Emma says something to me on the way out and I don't even stop. I can't. Everything I know is spinning around and around in my head. I have brothers. Plural. Three other men out there in the world that I share blood with and have never even met.

The thoughts torment me for the rest of the night.

By the next day, I've worked up a pretty good rage. It's the Irish genes, my mom always says. I'm not sure about that because my brother Finn is the exact opposite. Well, he used to be the exact opposite. Before he came back from war with a busted leg and found his fiancée with another man.

I park my bike in one of the spaces labeled with Finn's number. The old Ford pickup he's had for years sits next to me. I tuck my helmet under my arm and ride the elevator to the top floor. He's in Penthouse B, which faces the West side of the building. He didn't have the same ethical dilemma with accepting the old man's largesse. Finn has always seen the world in black and white. In his words, "If the bastard wants to give me money, I'll let him." That's my brother, the diplomat.

I use my key and enter his spacious apartment. The rancid smell of old takeout and funky gym shoes hits me as soon as I push the door open.

"Finn? Are you here?"

I call out to him out of courtesy not because I think he's actually gone. He hasn't left the place to my knowledge in several weeks. Not since he moved in. I pass through the kitchen. It's a fucking mess with bottles, empty paper plates and pizza boxes everywhere. I pick up an empty container that smells like fried rice, disturbing the family of flies nesting there.

“Finn?”

"What do you want, Tank?" His voice comes from the general direction of the living room.

He's sitting on the couch, his leg propped up on the coffee table. I've learned to control my expressions around Finn but there's no doubt that I'm shocked every time I see him. His leg is shriveled, easily half the size it should be. It looks so fragile next to the rest of his body. We have the same deep brown eyes but his hair is lighter than mine, almost blond. It looks darker now, and hangs in dirty clumps all over his head, like it hasn't been washed in a while. When he looks at me, his cheekbones appear even more sunken than last week. He's lost more weight.

"I went to the lawyer’s office yesterday. I signed the papers."

He closes his eyes and looks happier than he has in weeks. "Good. You deserve that money. Maybe you can finally take a break. Do whatever it is normal people do. Go sit your big ass on a beach somewhere."

I laugh because I know he expects me to. It's a bitter, strangled sound. "I wouldn't even know what to do on a beach. I'd probably shoot the first seagull that landed near me."

He laughs again and then his face twists into a mask of pain. "Pills are wearing off."

I stand. "I'll get them."

His apartment is top of the line, granite counters, recessed lighting and cherry wood cabinets. The first thing he did with his money was buy this apartment building. It'll generate a nice profit for him every quarter and he won't have to worry about money while he's recuperating.

I would feel a lot better about his mental state if he were actually *doing* something to recuperate. Instead he's been sitting in the midst of all this finery slowly letting his life and his body go down the drain.

His medications are lined up on the counter. The first bottle contains the painkillers his doctor prescribed. It's almost empty so I know he's been taking these. I glance back to where Finn is on the couch. I suspect that he's taking more of them than he's supposed to. The others are things I can't pronounce. I shake out the required number of each and carry them along with a glass of water back to the couch. I set it all down on the glass top next to his foot.

"Don't you get tired of this? Babysitting me?"

When I don't answer, he heaves a sigh and leans forward to grab the handful of pills. It pains me to see the strain and effort it costs him to move. He throws the entire handful in his mouth and then downs the glass of water in one big mouthful.

"Babysitting comes with the territory. It's Big Brother 101." The statement makes me think of what the lawyer told me. "Did you know about the others?"

Finn collapses back against the cushions of the couch. "Other what?"

"Our other brothers. According to Stevens, there are five of us total." The names I saw in that file have been swimming around in my head ever since. Gabriel. Zachary. Lucas.

"I didn't know. Maybe he told me and I just wasn't paying attention. I was pretty out of it." Finn looks vaguely embarrassed.

I think back to the half-empty bottle of pain pills. He must have been in one of his fogs that day.

"If we're going to do this, we'll have to meet them. I'm not sure how I feel about that. But it's a lot of money. It could really help Mom."

"If it can help her, then I say we do it. Plus, aren't you curious? We have brothers. I wonder what they're like."

I have to concentrate not to grind my teeth. "Probably just like him. I wonder if they're the reason he was never around. Too busy playing house with his new and improved family, I bet."

"Maybe." Finn shrugs and I can tell the pills are kicking in. His eyes glaze over and the strain on his face smoothes out until he looks blissful.

I get up and cover him with the blanket on the side of the couch.

He sleeps out here most of the time. He says the nightmares don't happen as much when he's upright. I've never asked him what he saw overseas that haunts him so. A man's demons should be his own.

"I'll check on you later, bro." He doesn't stir as I let myself out.

By the time I reach the parking deck, the cold has penetrated the outer layers of my leather jacket, icy teeth burrowing into my skin. I welcome the discomfort. It keeps me sharp. Normally I'd go visit my mom and make sure she has everything she needs but in light of recent events, I'm not sure what to do.

Does she know about my brothers? Should I tell her? Things were over between her and my dad ages ago. But that doesn't mean she'll want to hear about kids he had with some other woman. Or is it other *women*? Shit. I didn't even think to ask. Just how many families does the bastard have out there in the world?

The last thing I want is to dump these worries on my mom's doorstep. She's had more than her fair share of worry over the years between scraping to survive while we were growing up, to all the years I gave her hell as a teenager with my bad attitude and all the fighting. If she knew about the things I've been doing lately … I push the thought away. I deal with my anger in my own way. My mom has earned the right to a little peace, although fate doesn't seem inclined to give it to her.

I bury the ugly thoughts as I climb on the back of my Ducati. The last thing I want is to crash my bike. I run my hands over the custom paint job, the black shining even in the darkness. There's a cherry red stripe down the center that looks like a tongue. It's the only thing I've really spent any money on. I chuckle at the thought. Finn bought an investment property and I bought a bike.

Who's the responsible one, now?

Chapter Three

Emma

I step out of my car and hand the valet the keys. He's looking at my car with barely veiled disgust. Even I have to admit my twelve-year-old economy car looks ridiculous in front of this fancy hotel. The valets here probably make more in tips each day than this car is worth.

The elevator bank is behind the reception desk so I skirt the people standing in line and step directly into an open car. I've delivered letters to Mr. Marshall a few times now so I know where to go. Patrick trusts me to deliver them and that feels good. He only gave me this job because he knew my dad and he feels sorry for me but I'm determined to prove to him that he made the right decision. That he can trust me.

The woman who answers the door of Mr. Marshall's hotel suite perks up when she sees me. She's usually here when I visit. "Miss Shaw. Hello, again. Mr. Marshall is expecting you."

It was such a surprise the first time I came when Maxwell Marshall greeted me himself. Working for Patrick these past six months, I've learned a lot about the über rich. Very rarely do they sit and chat with the help.

But Mr. Marshall is different. He always seems genuinely pleased when I come by. He actually reminds me of some of the older people at the nursing home where my grandma spent her last days. They were so excited to talk to anyone who would listen. It always broke my heart to see them like that, starved for contact, so grateful for any companionship that they'd accept any they could get.

I've been visiting him each week now, even when I don't have a delivery. I've seen the looks I get from his staff. No doubt they wonder what a grizzled old billionaire and a young college student could have in common. But surprisingly, there's a lot.

For one thing, family.

My parents are gone and Mr. Marshall is trying to reconnect with his estranged relatives. I didn't ask too many questions but I'm pretty sure Tank Marshall is the one giving him the most trouble. Each week that Tank comes in to the office, I bring Mr. Marshall a package that makes him look sadder and sadder. Tank seems like the arrogant type so I shouldn't be surprised. But I can't imagine why anyone wouldn't at least give an elderly grandparent the benefit of the doubt. Mr. Marshall has mentioned several times that all he wants is to reconnect with his family.

He turns when I enter the room, wheeling himself over next to the couch. "Miss Shaw. It's always a pleasure. I hope you have time for some tea. How are your college applications coming?"

He looks good today. The deep hollows in his cheeks have filled out some and the tufts of white hair on his head have all been brushed in the same direction.

I slip my coat off and sit on the edge of the couch. "I'm still considering my options. Everything is so expensive. I took your advice and applied for some grants. I got some but not enough. So, I'll start searching for internships next. Maybe I can get one that pays something and offers college credit. Two birds, one stone."

He leans forward, a wide smile on his face. "Excellent news! I'm glad my thoughts on the matter were helpful."

I look around expectantly. Suddenly he laughs. "He'll be here in a moment."

We're interrupted by the frantic scratching of nails on carpet. Buddy, his five year old bulldog, races across the carpet and crashes into my leg. He looks up at me in excitement, his tongue hanging out of his mouth.

"Buddy! Where have you been?"

Mr. Marshall watches us with amusement. "My assistant was giving him a treat. I know the real reason you love coming here so much and it's not to see this grumpy old man."

I can't hide my smile as I scoop up Buddy and settle his plump bottom on my lap. He wiggles against me unable to contain his pleasure at the cuddle. I scratch behind his ears. "Did you miss me, boy?"

He contents himself nuzzling in my hand for a while and then once he's convinced that I don't have food, he curls up in my lap with his head on his paws.

"He always seems to know when you're coming. Animals do have a sixth sense, don't they?" Mr. Marshall says.

"Yes, they do. Oh, I brought some documents from Mr. Stevens." I hand over the sealed envelope I've carried in my oversized handbag. I can only hope that this one won't dim the smile on his face. He's in a jovial mood and I would hate to see it ruined.

"Aaah, I see my son has finally responded." Mr. Marshall gazes at the papers he's withdrawn from the envelope with satisfaction.

"Your son?"

He slides the papers back in the envelope and deposits it on the edge of the coffee table. "Yes, Tanner Marshall."

"Tank is your son?"

He looks up at my shocked inquiry. "Yes, strange I know. I'm not sure how an ugly bastard like me managed to produce so many fine-looking young men but somehow I did."

Heat rushes to my face. "Oh that's not what I meant at all, sir."

I was actually shocked because Mr. Marshall is so much older. I had assumed he was a grandparent or a distant cousin looking up his long-lost relatives. Patrick never discusses the particulars with me, which I understand completely. Dealing in estate law, part of his job is to be discreet.

"But he is a good-looking boy, isn't he?"

I look up when I realize he's talking to me. "Tank? Yes, he is."

Honestly good-looking seems like a tepid comparison when trying to describe someone like Tank. It's not that he's handsome. His features are too stark and far too masculine to be considered conventionally attractive. He's, well … *larger-than-life*, seems to be as good as I can do.

"My other sons have proven much easier to deal with so far. Tanner, he always was difficult."

"I'm sorry, sir. I'm sure he'll come around."

"I don't have much time left. Time has gotten away from me. Although I suppose everyone thinks that. I've made a lot of mistakes but this, this is something I can fix. I just need him to give me the chance."

"Your son, he's a very forceful man. I don't think he's used to taking orders from anyone. He doesn't seem to take no well."

He wheels himself next to where I sit on the couch. "You sound like you know him well."

I realize that my words make it sound as if we're friends, which couldn't be further from the truth. He's an arrogant guy who probably flirts with every girl he comes in contact with and he seems to have a preoccupation with whether or not I eat dinner. My knowledge of him goes no further than that.

"No sir. I didn't mean to give that impression. He's just friendly when he comes in the office. That's all. If you don't mind me saying, your son is a bit of a flirt."

My words seem to delight him. "Oh yes. He's definitely my son. I've been a sucker for a pretty face more than a few times in my life. It's amazing what even a smart man will do for the right woman." He regards me for a few moments and then wheels himself over to the window. Then he turns himself around so he's facing me again.

"I'm going to make you an offer, Miss Shaw. You are in the unique position of being able to help me with something that I want more than just about anything else."

"Well, I'll try to help if I can. What do you need me to do?"

"Have you ever heard of lobbying?"

I nod. I've never been interested in politics but I paid attention in Civics class. "Yes, lobbyists are paid to promote certain interests. They speak on behalf of certain industries or causes to influence lawmakers."

"Exactly. They're spokespeople carrying a message. I need you to carry a message for me. A very important message. You're a pretty girl, Miss Shaw. Most men are willing to listen when a message is carried by a lovely face."

He steeples his hands in front of him. His eyes roam over me and for the first time in his presence, I'm uncomfortable.

"Convince my son to meet with me and I'll pay you more than enough to cover all your schooling. One million dollars."

I put my teacup down on the table gently. My hand is shaking. I'm waiting for the punch line but when I look up at him, his eyes are clear and his expression completely open.

He's serious.

"That's utterly ridiculous. Why would you pay so much … for what? For me to carry a message?"

Buddy whimpers suddenly and I realize I've curled my nails into his fur. I soothe him with a gentle caress and a pat. He settles back down.

"Well, it's a little more than that. I'm understating the gravity of the situation when I say that my son refuses to meet with me. It would be more accurate to say that he loathes my very existence and would prefer to pretend I don't exist. If you can change his mind, then I'll consider a million to be a bargain."

"There's a chance that given some time he'll come around on his own. Don't you think you should just, I don't know, wait?"

"Time. The one thing I don't have any more of." His eyes cloud and I remember then that he is sick. And I feel an unmistakable tug of pity.

"I'm not sure what you think I can do. But I'll ask him."

"He'll respond better if he doesn't know the suggestion is coming from me."

It feels so sleazy, the thought of trying to convince Tank to come see his dad without him knowing why. It's not like we're friends. How would I even bring that up in conversation? But we're talking about a lot of money. It could mean the difference between working two jobs for years trying to earn tuition money and going to college in a few months. It could mean moving out of the house and into a place of my own. No more struggling.

No more Jon.

"I realize this is unorthodox but this is a job offer, Miss Shaw. No more, no less. It's a legitimate job offer that can give you the money you need to fulfill your dreams. Veterinary school is expensive. You could finish your studies with no debt hanging over your head. No worries. Think of the possibilities."

His eyes gleam and there's a maniacal light in his eyes that I've never seen before. Suddenly, it's all too much. Too much pressure and too much to think about.

"I'm not sure I can do what you're asking. Not that Tank would listen to me anyway. I'll let you know." I stand and gather my things.

He dips his head in acknowledgment. "Fair enough. All I want you to do is try. There's no harm in that."

* * * * *

Later that evening I'm still chewing on Mr. Marshall's offer. I don't have much time to think though because my car wouldn't start again and I had to ask Ivy for a ride to my second job.

Now I'm late.

As I trot across the gravel parking lot toward the back entrance of the Black Kitty, my tote bag bounces against my side. The neon sign isn't lit up yet. Without the blinking sign it could almost pass for a regular bar instead of a strip club.

Lou, the bouncer, holds the door open for me. "He's in a mood tonight. Try to stay out of his way. And he told me to tell you the new uniforms start tonight."

He is Paul Lattimer, the owner of the Black Kitty and a first-rate dirtbag. He thinks because he owns this club that he owns all of us who work here, too. But as much as I'd like to tell him to shove it, I need this job.

I let out a long sigh. "Great. Just what I needed. Thanks for the warning."

The lights on the stage are already on and I give an absent wave to Carina, one of the bartenders, as I pass. I drop my tote bag on the bench in front of my locker and tug my shirt out of my jeans. There's nothing quite like the hustle and bustle backstage before a show. Undressing in front of other people is still a little weird honestly but after a few months working here, it doesn't faze me like it used to. I never thought I'd be accustomed to the sight of half-naked girls walking around wearing nothing more than a thong and some pasties, but such is life.

This is my new normal.

"Are you almost ready?" My friend Sasha sits down on the wooden bench next to me.

As usual, she's decked out in a long evening gown and her hair is styled in intricate little braids that frame her face perfectly. The smell of the hot lemon water she drinks before every performance wafts up from the small paper cup in her hand. She looks different tonight. Tense.

"I'll be fine. They're just boobs, right? Not like I'll be showing them anything they haven't seen before." It's kind of pathetic that I'm so worried about this. I'm just a waitress here so most of the guys aren't looking at me.

"You don't have to pretend like it doesn't bother you. I know you better than that," Sasha declares.

The thing is, she's right. It does bother me. I actually have nothing against nudity as long as it isn't *mine*. Maybe if I had more confidence, *or more cleavage*, I think as I look down at my small chest, I'd be okay with this. Lou tried to convince me to get on stage when I first started working here but I shut that down early. I was blushing for the first week straight as it was just because of the short skirts we wear. No one wants to see me hyperventilate if I were to get on stage and undress.

There's nothing sexy about cardiac arrest.

Sasha moves closer and puts her arm around my shoulders. For just a moment, I lean in. It's been so long since I've had a comforting hug. Then I immediately feel guilty for the thought. It's not like I'm completely alone in the world. I have Ivy.

"Okay, I have to confess." Sasha squeezes my shoulder. "I did something. You're probably going to be mad at me, but I don't care."

"You didn't say anything to Lattimer, did you? I'll get fired."

She shakes her head, her long black braids swinging gently around her face. "No, I didn't talk to that little weasel. But he might wish I had once my friends get done with him."

Sasha's best friend is marrying some guy who owns a security company. The way Sasha describes it, he basically commands his own private army. She's been threatening to call in a squadron of bodyguards for a few weeks now. I didn't think she'd actually do it.

"This is only going to make things worse. He's going to be pissed."

It's not like I didn't know this was a strip club when I started. I'm used to waiting tables and letting drunk guys feel me up in exchange for tips. But Lattimer has suddenly decided that I need to fit in more with the other waitresses. I've always been able to wear my black skirt and short belly top.

Now he wants me to wear *this*.

I look down at the bikini top in my hand. It's yellow and sparkly, sending iridescent beams of light back up into my eyes. It shouldn't be such a big deal. People wear less sunbathing at the beach. Well, not me. I've always worn one-piece suits.

"You're not the only reason I called him," Sasha whispers. She avoids my eyes and takes a small sip from her cup. Steam curls up between us in little wisps.

"Did he threaten you?" I whisper.

The thought of Lattimer bullying her fills me with helpless rage. Sasha is one of the only girls here who stands up to him. As a result, he singles her out more than the others when he's on one of his tirades.

"Yeah but I can handle him. It's the rest of you guys I'm worried about. I've seen the way he looks at you, Em."

Something inside me shrivels up at just the thought. He's easily old enough to be my father. My thoughts must be written clearly on my face because Sasha suddenly bursts out laughing. "If you could see your face right now!"

I start giggling, too. I'm sure my face probably looked like I'd just bitten into a lemon because that's how I feel when I think of him. Like I have a sour taste in my mouth that I can't get rid of.

"But seriously, I know you haven't said anything because you need the job but no one should have to put up with this crap for a paycheck. Someone needs to put him in his place. And luckily I know just the guy for the job."

"Your friend's boyfriend must be pretty scary."

Sasha makes a small murmur of agreement. "Yeah, he's pretty intense. Lattimer is probably going to pee his pants. I must admit I'm looking forward to watching Eli make that little worm squirm."

I bump her shoulder lightly. "Thanks, Sasha."

She grins back at me and yanks the yellow sequins out of my hand. "You're welcome. And you're not wearing this one. Come on. I have some time before my set. If you're going to show a little more skin, let's find something that doesn't make you look like a broken stoplight."

Chapter Four

Tank

I’m about to pull off when my phone vibrates against my side. It's buried in the inner pocket of my leather jacket. I pull it out and stare at the screen.

Eli Alexander.

"Hey boss, miss me already?"

I'm joking but in a way I'm not. My boss and I are pretty tight. He gave me a job when I wasn't sure what the hell I was going to do with myself. My Army Special Forces training doesn't exactly line up with any of the typical job listings. Recon, tracking people, shooting shit, I'm your guy. I wasn't sure how I was going to fit into a typical nine-to-five situation when Elliott gave me a job with his private security firm.

"Tank? Hey, how are things with your brother?"

I didn't tell Eli the full truth about why I needed time off. He knows my brother hasn't been doing well and that my mom has been in the hospital. I left out the part about Daddy Warbucks. I figured that was too weird to share.

"He's doing about the same. I just left his apartment after making him take his meds."

"Sorry, that sounds rough. If you need more time, just let me know. Actually, I was calling to see if you had time to do a job. Off the books."

I sit up straight. My boss is a straight arrow type, most of the time. Of course some of the stuff I overheard on our last job has proven that he has secrets just like everyone else. "What's the job?"

"Kay has a friend who's being harassed by her boss. I just wanted you to look in on her. Make sure she's okay. Bust a few heads if you have to but I'd rather you keep your hands clean if possible."

"Who's the friend?" I can hear the edge in my voice as I ask the question.

“It’s Sasha. I know you two don’t exactly get along.”

"Aw hell. She hates me. Sending me there is bound to just piss her off."

"I know the last time you saw her things were tense but I think she'll be glad to see you now. Kay says things are pretty bad. I think her boss has been pressuring her to do more than sing, if you know what I'm saying. And he's doing the same thing to some of the other girls, too."

Eli did a background check on me before I was hired so I'm sure he knows my mom was a stripper back in the day. I grew up in and out of clubs like the Black Kitty so I have some personal history with the kind of men who run them. And if Sasha's boss is pressuring her for anything she's not willing to give, I'll consider it a public service to introduce his face to my knuckles.

"I'll do it," I say quietly.

"Thank you. Sorry to bother you while you're off but I'm in D.C. this week wrapping up some stuff and Kay just told me. I'd love to take care of it myself but thanks. I'll owe you one."

"Trust me, it'll be my pleasure."

After we hang up, I start my bike and strap on my helmet. The Black Kitty is the next city over, Virginia Beach, so it won't take long to get there.

The traffic is light and I weave in and out of lanes to reach the club. It's nothing more than an old warehouse that's been converted. It looks like a tin box sitting in the middle of a gravel parking lot. I stow my helmet on the back of my bike and walk past the line of people waiting to get in. One of the guys backs up a step and bumps into me.

"Hey, watch it!" He takes one look at me and holds up his hands. "Oh … sorry dude. My bad."

I keep walking until I reach the front of the line. There's a guy manning the door who's the size of a mountain wearing huge diamond earrings. His pale head gleams bald under the neon lights over the door.

"You must be Tank. I'm Lou. Sasha's in the back getting dressed. Once her number is over, she'll meet you at the bar."

I wonder briefly how he knew it was me, and then realize Eli must have called him. We shake hands and he stands back to allow me to enter. Several people in the long line waiting to get in make disgruntled noises but when I turn to face them, the entire line goes silent.

"The guy who owns this club, Lattimer, he's a real piece of work. I've seen the way he treats some of the girls and I don't like it. If you need any help, I've got your back."

"Thanks man." I cross through the dim entrance and into the body of the club. It looks like any other bar at first glance, bad techno music, alcohol flowing and guys hitting on girls who aren't nearly drunk enough to go home with them yet.

"Tank! What are you doing here?" Sasha doesn't exactly look happy to see me but at least she's not hitting me with her purse this time.

"Eli sent me."

She nods and hops up onto the bar stool next to me. She's wearing a long gold dress covered in some kind of sparkly shit. I know nothing about women's clothes but I can definitely appreciate that it dips low in the back exposing a ton of caramel colored skin. She's a beautiful girl with high cheekbones, big brown eyes and long braided dark hair. If Finn were here, he'd be all over her. He's always been a ladies' man.

"Thanks for coming. Things have been pretty bad lately."

"So where is this fucker?" I scan the other people at the bar. The bartender is at the other end, pouring colorful drinks and chatting with the two girls leaning over the bar flirtatiously.

"He's in the back. He usually doesn't make his appearance until the end." She leans closer, glancing around before she says, "He's been making threats, telling a lot of the girls they'll be let go if they don't *accommodate* him. My friend was backstage on the verge of tears. She's just waitressing here trying to earn tuition money. She shouldn't have to deal with this crap. Oh, look here she comes. Emma!"

I can feel it before I even turn around. Somehow I just know it's her. There's a shift in the air and then she's there, standing next to me, chatting with Sasha. My eyes land on her costume or lack thereof. She's wearing the tiniest skirt I've ever seen and a little bikini top that pushes her breasts up like ripe fruit. It's covered in purple sequins.

When her eyes finally land on me, she makes a sound that's a cross between a groan and a squeak. "Tank? Oh my god." She crosses her arms over her chest and the tray she's carrying falls to the ground. Automatically, I bend to retrieve it which puts me right on eye level with the cleavage.

Hell.

* * * * *

Time stretches between us painfully as Sasha looks back and forth between us warily. "You two know each other?"

"No."

"Yes."

We both speak at the same time. Emma looks appalled. Her hands are still covering the front of her bikini top and from the death glare on her face, I'll lose an eye if my gaze drops anywhere below her neck. It requires a remarkable amount of self-control on my part because the one look I got was spectacular.

Which of course means I can't help messing with her a little.

"*Emma Shaw*. Is that you? You look … different somehow. I almost didn't recognize you."

She growls and points a finger at my chest. "What are you doing here? Are you stalking me now?" The movement exposes the left side of her chest and I'm almost blinded by sparkly purple sequins. I blink and when she notices my gaze, she yanks her hand down covering her chest again.

"I'm doing what every other red-blooded American guy does on a random Tuesday night. Having a beer at a club. Visiting a friend."

Sasha is watching us with a knowing grin. "So how do you two know each other?"

Emma doesn't respond so I answer. "I asked Eli to recommend an estate lawyer."

Sasha grins. "And let me guess, he recommended Patrick Stevens? Yeah, that makes sense. I've done temp work there off and on for several years. That's how I met Emma, actually. Kay's family uses him and now Eli does, too. Small world, huh?"

"Yeah. Small world." I take another sip of my beer, watching Emma adjust the tiny top shielding her breasts from view.

A girl wearing a peacock headdress, sparkly red high heels and a red thong runs up to us. "Sasha, where have you been? You're on next!"

"Oh crap. I have to go. Thanks for coming again Tank. I really appreciate it. Emma, you stay here and keep Tank company while I'm on stage." Sasha gathers up the edges of her long dress and then rushes after the peacock girl, leaving Emma and I alone in uncomfortable silence.

The music is pretty loud and for once, I'm grateful for the eardrum splitting decibel level of the music.

Emma snatches the tray I'm holding. "I'm still on the clock. I have to work."

"Okay. Don't let me hold you. I'm going to stick around until after Sasha's set. Can you do me a favor?"

"What?" She narrows her eyes.

"If you see the asshole who's been bothering Sasha, point him out to me."

Her eyes gleam in the shifting colors of the strobe lights on the stage, reflecting blue, orange, and red. She nods quickly. "I will definitely do that. He always walks the floor around eleven o'clock."

"Give me your phone."

She reaches into her pocket and pulls out an ancient flip phone. I take it from her fingers and dial my own number. Then I hang up.

"Text me when you see him."

She stares at me for a long moment, and then nods. I watch the sway of her hips as she walks away.

For the next hour, I listen as Sasha sings everything from jazz standards to covers of popular songs. She has a soft, sultry voice that throbs in your blood and makes you think of twisted sheets and a different kind of rhythm all together. My phone buzzes and I pull it out.

- - - He's here. In the red suit.

I look behind me. Emma is standing a few tables away. When she catches my eye, she nods her head to the right. There's a short man with a tragic comb-over walking on the edge of the dance floor. Two large men follow him. I toss back the last of my beer and get up to follow him.

"Are you Lattimer?"

He takes a step forward and his goons crowd in closer, too. I stand to my full height and flex beneath my jacket. It only takes a glance to tell that these two won't be a problem but Eli asked me to keep it clean. So, I'm hoping to avoid a fight.

"Who wants to know?"

"I'm a friend of Sasha's. I'm just here checking things out. I look out for her. Make sure no one bothers her."

"Did she say someone was bothering her?"

"I wanted to see for myself."

He comes closer and his goons follow. They're crowding around me. One of the bodyguards cracks his knuckles. It takes everything I have not to laugh in his face. The most lethal people I've ever met don't need to posture and show off. If you cross them, you'll be dead and never see them coming.

"Not so tough now, huh?" Lattimer boasts. He pushes me in the chest and then frowns when I don't even move. But he recovers his tough guy attitude quickly. "This is my house. You don't come in here making threats at me in my own damn house."

Sasha comes up behind me. "Let's go, Tank. I don't want any trouble."

Lattimer scoffs. "You don't want any trouble? You've been trouble since the day you started here."

I don't turn around. Men like Lattimer only understand one thing. Force. I hold his eyes. He needs to understand that I have no problem fucking him up. That knowledge is the only thing that will keep him from screwing with her again.

One of his goons feints at me, trying to see if I'll jump back. I can't help it, I react on instinct, punching him in the throat and then following it with a gut shot. He falls back and knocks into his boss. They both crash into the table behind him.

Sasha gasps and covers her mouth with her hands. I groan and run my hands through my hair. She's really going to hate me now.

"Shit. Sorry. I shouldn't have done that. Eli said to scare him not to start a fight."

She turns to me, her brown eyes suddenly bright with excitement. "Are you kidding? That was *awesome*."

Lattimer stumbles to his feet, knocking into the guys sitting at the table who are obviously drunk. One of them punches wildly at one of the bodyguards. Before long the panic spreads and we're in the middle of a crowd of people pushing and shoving. I've been in enough bar fights to know that most of the people throwing punches don't even know what's going on.

"Ouch! Get your hands off me."

Emma is caught between a group of guys who are trying to take each other down. She's jostled back and forth and then stumbles to the side. I push through the crowd, shoving anyone in front of me out of the way. When I reach her, I push her behind me just as one of the guys swings out wildly, his fist connecting with my side.

I block his next punch and then shove him back. His buddies apparently want in on the action now because they've focused on me. The chill I always feel before a good fight settles over me. The next one charges me. I dip low and catch him at the waist, flipping him onto his back. My arms and hands move in a violent dance, punching, blocking and knocking heads together. After the first three go down, the rest of their buddies back away slightly.

Emma whimpers behind me. I reach back and pull her against my back, using my body as a shield to block her from the crowd. Fights still rage around us. Sasha appears at my elbow. "Let's get out of here. This is crazy."

Lattimer finally gets up, brushing away the offer of help from his other bodyguard. The guy holds his throat while glaring at me. He looks between the three of us and then sneers. "All of you need to get the hell out of my club."

"What? Paul, that is not fair. Emma has *nothing* to do with this. And a bunch of drunks fighting is not my fault." Sasha glares at him.

"I don't care. I don't need this shit. Both of you get out and don't bother coming back."

Sasha points at him. "This is really messed up and you know it. Just wait, karma is a bitch with a really long memory. And she has your address now."

Sasha holds out a hand to Emma. "We're going to get our stuff from the back."

I follow them, standing guard at the entrance to the dressing room and keeping an eye on Lattimer and his goons. They watch us but don't attempt to come closer or prevent the girls from getting their stuff. Sasha emerges wearing black leggings and an oversized red sweater. Emma has changed into a plain white blouse with ruffles on the front and hip hugging jeans.

"Come on. Let's get out of here."

I follow them out to the parking lot.

Emma stops in the middle of the gravel lot. "Crap, I forgot that I didn't bring my car today. I need to call my sister for a ride. She wasn't expecting me to be out this early."

Sasha holds up her keys. "I can take you."

"I don't want you to have to drive out of your way."

I stop next to my bike. I'm suddenly grateful that I bought the extra helmet. "Where do you live? I'll take you home."

Emma regards me warily. "In Norfolk. Near the shipyard."

I wave her over. "That's not that far from me. We'll follow

Sasha home to make sure she gets there safely. Then I'll take you home."

"Okay. Thanks." She adjusts the strap on her bag and then takes the helmet I hand her. I adjust the strap for her and then climb on the bike. She eyes it like some strange beast she's never seen before.

"Climb on. It won't bite. And neither will I."

Her eyes narrow but she climbs on the back. She's holding me gingerly around the waist. I start the engine and she squeals and grabs me tighter.

Now that's better.

We pull out, following Sasha's car. I already know her address from when I was on her friend Kaylee's security detail but it's been a while since I've been there. Plus it's harder to concentrate on directions when I have Emma snugged against my back, her thighs gripping mine. She catches the rhythm of riding quickly, leaning with me on the turns.

All too soon, we pull up in front of Sasha's apartment building. Emma climbs off and then removes the helmet. Her cheeks are flushed.

"Your first time?"

She looks startled for a moment then her cheeks go red. "Yeah, I've never ridden before."

"If I could only read minds right now."

She flushes again and turns to follow Sasha. I know I should stop teasing her but I can't help it. It's so easy.

"Are you okay, Sasha?"

Sasha shrugs. "I was expecting him to fire me, but I wasn't trying to get you fired, too. I'm really sorry."

"I don't care. I can find another crappy job."

Sasha turns to me. "Tank, do you mind coming in for a minute. I'm still pretty rattled. I don't want to be alone just yet."

"Of course."

We step inside and Sasha locks the door and slides the chain in place. Then she turns to Emma. "Em, your mascara is running. Why don't you use my bathroom? I have makeup remover beneath the counter that you can use."

As soon as Emma turns the corner out of sight, Sasha grabs my arm and drags me into the kitchen. "Look we don't have long so I just needed to warn you. Em lives with her sister but I think something happened. She's crashed on my couch a couple of times but I think she's worried about being here too much. It's a pride thing. Knowing her she'll probably let you drop her off at home and then leave as soon as she thinks you're gone."

A door opens in the hallway. Sasha lets go of my arm just as Emma turns the corner into the kitchen.

"Wow, I really did look like a raccoon. Thanks for warning me, Sasha. I would have hated to go home looking like that. I'd never hear the end of it."

"Why don't you stay here? You can crash on the couch and then I can drive you to work in the morning."

Emma smiles tightly. "No, I need to get home. Ivy will worry otherwise." She glances at me. "Ivy is my older sister."

"Oh, well, okay then. I guess you guys should get going then." Sasha gives me a look as soon as Emma turns around. I nod, so she knows that I got the message.

I'm not sure if Emma would try to trick me but if she does, she won't get far.

Chapter Five

Emma

As soon as Sasha closes the door behind us, I stop walking. Tank stops too and stares at me. I cross my arms and try to drum up some bravado.

"You're not going to tell Mr. Stevens, are you?"

"What? No, why would I do that?"

Relief sweeps through me. It's not that I thought he would tell, it's just that I can't take any chances. Mr. Stevens is a conservative guy and he's already gone out on a limb by hiring me in the first place. The last thing I want to do is give him any reason to question that decision.

"I don't know. I just had to be sure. I need that job. Especially now that I just lost my second income."

Tank's face doesn't change but somehow I sense that I've offended him with the question. "I wouldn't do that, Emma. It's your secret to keep. Although you haven't done anything wrong and have nothing to be ashamed of. Now where am I taking you?"

I give him the address and then climb on the back of his motorcycle. He waits for me to adjust the helmet before he pulls out. I can tell he's holding back for my sake. As strange as it seems, I wish he'd go faster. Really let loose. I want to know what it feels like to do something a little crazy. But true to form, I don't ask him to. I just squeeze my arms tighter around his middle and lean against his back.

He pulls up outside of the house. My heart sinks when I see the blue muscle car sitting next to Ivy's silver sedan. Jon is here.

I climb off the bike, awkwardly and hand Tank the helmet. "Thanks for the ride. And for what you did tonight. I know Sasha really appreciates it."

He flips up the front visor on his helmet. "I wish things had gone differently. My goal was to scare him, not get both of you banned."

I kick a loose pebble near my foot. I wish I could pretend that losing the job didn't matter. But the loss of that income is even more important now. Mr. Marshall's offer looms in my mind. One conversation with Tank and all my troubles could be over.

"I had to deliver a package to your father today."

His face immediately closes up. "Did you?"

"He's a nice old man. He always asks me about school and how things are going."

"Yeah, he's a model citizen all right. I'll wait until you get in the house before I take off."

Something must show on my face because his eyes narrow. I can tell he's about to say something else so I wave and walk toward the house. All I have to do is go inside and wait until he drives off. Then I can walk back to the law office. As soon as I close the front door behind me, I hear the sound of the motorcycle as he races off.

I take a quick shower and then stuff some fresh clothes in my bag. There's a soft thud against the wall that separates my room from the hallway. The door to my room is slightly ajar. I tiptoe to the door and peer through the crack out into the hallway.

Ivy stands in the living room, staring at her phone. Jon comes up behind her and she suddenly puts it in her pocket. I can't hear what they're saying but when Jon grabs her wrist and yanks her toward him roughly, I gasp. I cover my mouth with my hand but they don't seem to have heard me anyway. Ivy shoves Jon away and stalks back down the hall. He follows and then I hear her door slam.

After the way Jon behaved this morning and what I just witnessed, this is the last place I want to be. I stand in the doorway, for a moment, listening. They don't come back out so I grab my bag and head out. It's exactly twelve minutes later when I lock the front door behind me and skip down the front steps.

I want to weep at the thought of walking a little over a mile at this time of night. But my mind flashes back to this morning and I suddenly would rather be anywhere else. Jon has never been quite that blatant before. It's usually just the lecherous looks and the comments. I made the mistake of telling Sasha last week that Jon was hitting on me and wish I hadn't. She wasn't exactly subtle with her offer to crash on the couch tonight. But I don't need charity or to impose on my friends.

Contrary to what she thinks, I'm not all heartbroken and depressed because my sister is being such a bitch to me lately. There was a time when Ivy would have stood up for me. Before our parents died, she would have told Jon he could take her or leave her. But ever since then, she's been different. I've been different, too. I can hardly fault her for changing when I'm not the same person either.

It's eerily quiet as I pass the dark houses on my street. There's no one out this late. I hook the long strap of my messenger bag over my head so it doesn't get in the way. No doubt I'll have blisters by the time I get there but I should be able to curl up on the sofa in the waiting room and catch a few hours of sleep before Mr. Stevens comes in for the day. It's embarrassing enough that he knows I do it but to have him catch me would be even worse.

I turn the corner onto the main road. It borders a wooded area that always gives me the creeps. So when a dark shape moves out of the corner of my eye, I whirl around, my bag slapping me in the back of my thighs, fists at the ready.

"Going somewhere?"

Once it registers who it is, I scream in frustration. "Tank! What in the hell are you doing? You almost gave me a heart attack!"

"Where are you going, Emma?"

"None of your business."

He taps his fingers against the helmet resting on his thigh. "Is there some reason you don't want to go home?"

He's going to make me say it out loud. "Do you just get off on annoying me or what?"

"Something like that."

It's the lack of pity in his eyes that tears the words from my mouth. It's the understanding. Like he's been in my shoes a time or two and knows how much it sucks.

"My sister's boyfriend is there and he's just … I just, don't want to be there, okay?"

He nods, a quick perfunctory motion, like he was just waiting for me to finish so we could move on. "Get on."

"Wait, what? I just told you I'm *not* going back there."

He starts the engine and the loud sound startles me in the stark quiet of the night. "I know. You're coming home with me."

At any other time I would have a million arguments ready. I'd rail at him for making assumptions or make a joke about "what kind of girl do you think I am?"

But it's late. It's dark. And he represents the only safety I've had in a long, long time. So I do something that makes no sense.

I get on the back of his bike and wrap my arms around his waist.

"Okay. Let's go."

He pulls out and this time he's not holding back the way he did on the way here. Maybe he can sense the wildness growing inside me, the restless need I have to just feel. *Something*. Anything other than helpless. We arrive at an apartment building on the other side of town. He takes the helmet from me and stows it on the back of the bike. I follow him into the building and up several flights of stairs. We stop on the third floor. He unlocks it and then punches buttons on a keypad next to the door.

As we enter, his eyes are constantly moving, surveying the room and the hallway behind us. I can see why he's so good at his job. I get the sense that he's always on the alert for trouble.

"I like your place."

He narrows his eyes at me, as if searching to see if the comment is sincere or snarky. "There's nothing in here but a couch and a television."

I shrug. "Yeah, but it's yours. There's no one here to take your stuff or kick you out. I like it."

He sets his helmet on the kitchen counter and then drops down on the couch. "When you put it that way, I like it too. Do you want something to drink? I've got some sodas, fruit juice and I'm sure there's some bottled water somewhere. Or, are you hungry?"

I hold up a hand before he goes into a detailed account of the type of food he has here. All I really want is to crash but I'm not exactly sure how this is going to work. His couch looks really comfortable but he's sitting there now and doesn't look like he's planning on moving anytime soon.

"Truthfully, I'm exhausted. If I wait any longer, I'll fall asleep on my feet."

"Right. Follow me." He stands in one fluid movement and grabs my hand. I'm so stunned that I don't even yank it back. His palm engulfs mine and when I look down to where our fingers entwine, the size of his hand makes mine look like a child's.

"Let me just strip the sheets for you." He drops my hand as we enter a bedroom and I rub my palm absently, already missing the contact. Tank doesn't look like the kind of guy who does housework but he strips the bed of all the linen with the efficiency of someone who's done it a thousand times in his sleep. He disappears and I'm left standing next to the bed with nothing to do. Shouldn't I be helping?

I look at the book on the night table next to the bed. There's a picture of a soldier on the front. The comforter at my feet is a dark hunter green. The closet is open slightly, revealing several sets of fatigues and black combat boots. He hasn't come back yet so I wander over to the dresser and pull open the first drawer. It's filled with boxer briefs. I slam the drawer shut.

"Find what you were looking for?"

I turn around slowly. "This is your room!"

He laughs softly then bends to spread the clean sheets in his arms over the mattress. "What gave me away? My superior design skills or was it that warm, cozy feeling from the military fashions on display?"

"I didn't mean to kick you out of your own bed."

"Unless you're willing to share it then I'll be on the couch."

"I could take the couch. I'm smaller and I don't need as much room. That makes way more sense."

"Yeah, no."

I want to argue but then he picks up my hand and puts a folded towel and washcloth into my arms. My stomach tightens as our fingers brush. The warmth of his hands linger even after he lets go.

"There's no way I'm putting you on the couch. I've slept worse places, believe me. I'll be fine. Let me know if you need anything else." He backs away slowly, holding my gaze the entire time.

My blood heats at the intense look in his eyes. His shoulders are so broad they take up the entire doorway. All of a sudden, I remember him fighting off those guys. There was no hesitation on his part. He just jumped in front of me and took control of the situation. No one has ever done anything like that for me before.

Just before he hits the hallway, he says, "I'm glad you're here Emma."

I should be saying that to him. The weirdest thing is, I have the sense that he really is glad I'm there. We don't know each other that well and probably have nothing in common. He took out both of Paul's thugs tonight and a bunch of those drunk guys, too without breaking a sweat. I can't pretend his brutality doesn't scare me but he took those hits *for me*.

So in this moment, I've never felt safer in my life.

* * * * *

When I wake it's still dark and my heart picks up rhythm as I take in the unfamiliar environment. Then memory returns and I know where I am.

I'm with Tank.

Strangely enough, I'm completely comfortable. I smile at the thought. I never thought I'd be so comfortable in a random guy's bed. I turn over and collide with a warm, incredibly wide chest. A naked chest.

"Whoa, it's all right." Tank's deep voice grumbles through the darkness.

I should be pushing him away, climbing out of the bed. Instead I'm shocked into stillness. His hand travels up the bare skin of my arm and stops at the base of my neck. Goosebumps follow the path of his fingers. The man can turn me to mush with just one touch.

"What are you doing in here?" My voice comes out as a high-pitched squeak. He's so close that I can feel the soft puff of his breath against my hair. Part of me wishes it wasn't so dark so I could see for myself if he's just as built as he looks under all that leather.

"Don't get your panties in a twist. I have shorts on. You were having a nightmare."

"I was?" I wrap my arms around myself and curl up into a ball. I haven't had nightmares since my parents died. I used to dream of my mother and what she was wearing that day. All dressed up for a night on the town with my dad. You'd think the fact that she was so happy would be a comforting image. Instead, it tormented me for months that she could be so happy and have it all taken away in a matter of moments.

"Yeah. I wasn't trying anything, I swear. I just wanted to make sure you were okay. You seemed to sleep better with me here, so I stayed."

In my sleep-muddled state, I answer with more candor than I

otherwise would have. "What girl wouldn't sleep better next to you?"

His chest rumbles beneath my palm. "Miss Shaw, are you flirting with me?"

Before I can think of an answer, there's a soft snore. He's asleep again. The soft rumbling sound lulls me to sleep and I don't wake again until the next morning.

When I open my eyes, Tank is watching me. It's an odd thing to look at someone this close up. His dark hair is spiked up all over his head and his eyes are still heavy with sleep. He doesn't try to pretend like he's not looking either. His eyes take in the full image of my face and what I'm sure must be messy hair then down to where my breasts mold against the thin fabric of the T-shirt I borrowed.

Most of the girls who wait tables at the Black Kitty are used to those types of looks from men. Guys aren't that picky, especially when beer goggles are involved. They all do the same thing: they squint as they picture what's under your clothes and then there's that slightly glazed over look as they imagine what they'd do to you. It's usually the grossest feeling ever.

But with Tank, it's different. My body reacts immediately, my nipples blooming and pressing against the fabric. His gaze is like a touch; it awakens every one of my nerve endings. Heat blooms out from my core and spreads throughout me. Within moments I'm completely wet and ready for him.

"Were you watching me sleep?" I whisper.

When his eyes raise to mine, I see the answering desire there. There's a tension in his big body that tells me he can deliver on every inch of the promise his eyes are making.

"Good morning, buttercup." He kisses me softly, one hand sliding into my hair to cup my head. I'm so shocked that I don't do anything at first. Then he kisses me again and my hands drift up to his hair. I curl my fingers through the thick strands. He makes a soft sound in the back of his throat.

He likes that.

I pull him down on top of me and then my hands are in his hair again. He's so warm and everything about this feels so right. Waking up, sleepy and soft with this gorgeous hunk of man in my bed.

He shifts, allowing the full weight of his big body to press me into the mattress. It's all chemical, the insanely seductive way he smells, the erotic taste of his tongue in my mouth and the ache between my legs as he presses right up against my core. I'm burning up and surely he can feel it. My arms wrap around his shoulders and trace over the muscles that flex under my touch.

"I shouldn't be doing this," he mumbles. "But I'm no angel and you are so beautiful."

He inches down, his lips leaving soft kisses on my neck, my breastbone, then my stomach where the shirt I borrowed has ridden up. I squirm beneath the soft touches, especially as they get lower. His tongue dips into my belly button and then bites the swell below gently. I shudder under the assault, my hips pressing up with a will of their own.

He looks up at me, his eyes so dark and intense they look black. Then his head dips and his mouth settles over my sex.

"Tank!" I cry out again as he nips me through the fabric of my panties. He grabs the sides and pulls them down. The slide of the fabric against my skin is so erotic, especially when he sits back slightly and then looks at what's between my legs like he's never seen anything he wants as much. His eyes fall closed and he takes a deep inhale.

"I want your taste."

"Yes, please." I can't even think let alone understand anything he's saying. All I can see is that intense look in his eyes as he leans down and his tongue curls around my clit.

He settles himself between my knees, his big body pushing my legs out to make room for him. It's the most shameless feeling, being in his bed with my legs spread while he tongues me. But I'm not sure how much shame I have left, whatever I started with slowly dissolving as he pushes his tongue into my pussy. I can't do anything except splinter into a million pieces as he explores the lips of my sex and his hands cup my ass, pulling me forward for each thrust of his tongue.

I'm still shivering when he kisses my belly and then my neck. As he settles on top of me again, I soften beneath him, ready for him to strip my shirt off and finally have me completely naked. He kisses me and I can taste myself on his tongue. It just makes me hotter, sends my desire skyrocketing. I'm ready for him to make me come while he takes me. There's nothing I want more than to watch those incredible eyes as he finds his own pleasure.

I'm mindless and I want him to do something, anything that will put me out of this misery. But even as I arch under him, pressing upward, rubbing myself against him, he's slowing things down. The frantic coupling of our tongues changes to soft, suctioning kisses. His hands slide under my bottom but not to pull me closer, to hold me still.

"Tank, please." It should embarrass me that I'm essentially begging. But I've never felt this before, this all-consuming heat. This blinding desire to have him inside me. I've wanted men before but I've never felt this out of control. This needy.

"So sweet," he mutters. "So damn sweet."

He rolls to the side and pushes his face into the pillow next to me. I can hear his gasping breaths and I can definitely feel the iron-hard rod pressing against my thigh. What I don't understand is why he's stopped? Then as my heart rate slows down some, my reason returns. I put a hand over my mouth.

I just dry humped him like I was in heat.

"I'll get out of here so you can get ready." He pulls back and rolls over, presenting me with his back. I watch as he stands and then pulls on his jeans. Then he's gone.

* * * * *

This is the most awkward thing I've ever experienced. How do you handle a morning after that isn't really a morning after? Tank has now seen me with mascara trailing down my cheeks and hair that's snarled into a bird's nest of knots and we haven't even gone on a date.

After texting Ivy, I grab the towel and washcloth that Tank gave me last night and barricade myself in the bathroom. My hair is a wild tangle and I have little smudges of mascara beneath my eyes. I'm suddenly really grateful to Sasha for offering me her makeup remover last night. Clearly I didn't get it all but I hate to think of how bad I'd look this morning if I had gone to sleep in full war paint. I splash my face with water and then run my damp hands through my hair, trying to finger comb the tangles.

I don't have time for a long shower so I jump in and scrub at lightning speed. Then I dry off and towel dry my hair. There's a new toothbrush below the sink which I make use of and then do my best to slap some color into my cheeks. The makeup I wore yesterday was a lot heavier than the kind I have in my purse so I'll have to make do.

There's a soft knock at the door. "Emma? Let me know when you want me to take you home."

"Uh, just a second." God, this is embarrassing. I don't regret what happened this morning but it's definitely awkward since we're not dating. Or even friends. Now I'm supposed to talk to him like nothing happened?

After one last glance in the mirror, I open the door. Tank has dressed in jeans and a long sleeved black shirt. He looks edible. And so does the bagel he's holding out to me. I snatch it and take a huge bite. He chuckles.

"Yeah, I thought you might be hungry."

I'm slightly appalled at the way I attacked him for his food but I'm too hungry to care. "Starving. I didn't eat breakfast yesterday and my lunch was just a salad."

"What happened to dinner? This is why you need to go out with me. Clearly you don't understand the importance of the last meal."

I can't help but laugh. His determination is impressive. Plus, he has a point. But I can't think about that now.

"Anyway, I don't need a ride. My sister is coming to pick me up."

He's watching me carefully and it's obvious this is just as awkward for him as it is for me. It's strangely comforting that he doesn't know what to say. It would be worse if he was completely blasé about waking up with a random chick in his bed.

My phone beeps. "That's probably her now." I check my message and see that Ivy is waiting in front of the building. Part of me rails that the first time Ivy is on time for something is the one time I wish she was at least a little late.

"I've got to go. My sister is out front." I gather the few things from his room, my clothes from yesterday and fold them into my messenger bag.

Tank grabs his keys off the table near the front door. We ride down the elevator together in silence. Ivy is parked right in front of the building, illegally blocking in several cars. When she sees Tank, she rolls down the window and stares at him shamelessly. Her eyes widen when she gets a good look at him. The broad shoulders, the muscles. The sexily rumpled hair.

Crap. I need to get out of here before she says something inappropriate.

"If you ever need another rescue, or anything, let me know, okay?" Tank says, his dark eyes fixed on my face as he speaks.

I nod. Not sure what to really say to that. We aren't dating and we're not friends. Why would I call him? It was pure luck that he happened to be there last night and that was more for Sasha's benefit than mine.

"Thanks again, Tank. For everything." I give a little awkward wave and then hitch my messenger bag over my shoulder.

Ivy leans across the seat and pushes the passenger side door open. She opens her mouth to speak but Tank has already gone back into the building.

"What the hell, Emma? I heard you come in last night but then when I woke up this morning, you were gone."

"Sorry, yesterday was crazy. A fight broke out at the club and Lattimer has been out of control lately so Sasha has a friend who intervened. Unfortunately, we still got fired."

"I warned you that Paul was bad news. What did you expect working at that trashy club?"

"Great. Thanks Ivy. Way to blame the victim."

"I'm sorry, Em. I shouldn't have said that. Of course it's not your fault."

I let out a sigh. Ivy doesn't understand anything I do but I don't understand her choices any better. She seems to think dating a rich man solves all problems.

"I've been meaning to tell you, Jon has a friend that I think would be perfect for you. He's cute, too. You should let me fix you up."

"No way. I know you like Jon and he gives you nice gifts but that's not me, Ivy. I don't judge you but that's just not what I want out of life. I earn my own way. Do you remember how Mom used to give us those lectures before we went out on dates?"

Ivy's face softens. "*Get your own drinks. Pay your own way. And always have a way home.* Then she'd get that look and I'd know another sex talk was coming."

"Yeah. She was so proud of you when you went to college." Thinking about my mom always makes me a little sad but I want to be able to remember her without always seeing her the way she was at the end. Scared.

Ivy grips the steering wheel tighter. "Yeah."

"And then how she was so excited for me when I got that scholarship. She was almost more excited than I was. I wonder what she'd think of what I'm doing now. I guess she wouldn't be—"

"I can't talk about this with you!" Ivy shrieks.

The sudden outburst shocks me and the tears that have built up behind my eyelids suddenly spill over. She's the only one with these same memories but she won't talk to me about our parents. Ever. She won't talk about them at all.

After riding in silence for a few minutes, Ivy glances over at me. "Look, all I want is for you to be taken care of. Now you're dating this guy? I recognize him from the law office. I wouldn't be surprised if he was some kind of criminal. Seriously, Emma? It's time for you to stop playing around and get serious."

It's tempting to tell her just how wrong she is. She recognizes Tank but obviously never paid attention to his last name. If she knew how much money I've been offered to cozy up to Tank, she'd be all over me about it. Or she'd be all over Tank. Just the thought of that makes me itch.

"I am being serious. I still have my day job and I'm taking care of *myself*. I was just trying to earn extra money to save up for tuition faster but it's okay. I'll get the money another way."

"I hate to say this Emma but you need to face facts. We're alone now. There's no one to help us if we mess up. I'll try to help you but the things you used to wish for just aren't possible now."

"What are you talking about? There's still the money Mom and Dad left each of us. I was hoping to get more grants so I wouldn't have to use any of that but since I didn't, I don't have a choice. That's what they would have wanted anyway."

Her hands tighten on the steering wheel. "Oh Emma."

Something about the way she says it has me immediately on edge. "What? What's wrong now?"

She glances over at me and then back to the road. "Things were really hard after Mom and Dad died. The economy is bad and everybody is struggling. I didn't have any choice."

Even though my logical mind can see where this is going, I'm not ready to believe it. After everything else that has happened today I just can't handle hearing that all my college fund money is gone.

"How could it all be gone? What the hell, Ivy?"

"Don't blame me. You wanted to eat, too didn't you? Maybe

now you won't look down on me so much that you understand how hard it's been. You're an adult now and I can't keep shielding you from the truth. Reality is that we're broke. And broke people don't have the luxury of always staying on the straight and narrow because that doesn't keep food on the table. If school is what you want, you're going to have get more aggressive. Figure out how to take what you want."

My conversation with Mr. Maxwell floats through my mind. It seemed like such a seedy thing at the time. But in the end, how is it any worse than working at a strip club? Or what Ivy does, targeting rich men and seducing them? At least it's not illegal and doesn't involve me taking my clothes off.

Even though I technically had some of my clothes off earlier.

I shake my head to dispel the image of Tank's bare chest. Last night was an anomaly. Going forward, I won't be waking up in Tank's bed. There's no harm in inviting him out for the day and spending a little time with him. I can tell him about my visits with his dad, put in a good word and then let fate take care of the rest. Because Ivy is right. The money for my tuition isn't going to come from thin air.

And million dollar job offers don't come around very often.

Chapter Six

Tank

I don't have a lot of boundaries. This has gotten me into trouble a time or two in the past. So the thought occurs to me as I throttle my bike and merge onto the highway that running a background check on my brothers may not be exactly the right way to establish contact with them. It's foolish but in the end, I decide it's worth the risk.

I've had enough of surprises.

After Emma left, I couldn't seem to settle down. Her smell lingered all throughout my house, in the kitchen, on the towels in the bathroom and on my sheets. There was nowhere to go that I could escape from thoughts of her. Last night was supposed to be about protecting her but instead it just fed my fascination.

When she was here, I was calm. For the past two months, ever since my mom got her cancer diagnosis, I've felt out of control. Sleep is elusive and I haven't been able to find any productive way to channel the energy. When I was younger, I got into fights all the time. It was the only way to release the pent up anger I felt. After getting suspended multiple times, I'd come home to see my mom crying. She was overwhelmed working all the time and trying to figure out how to keep us boys out of trouble. It was the first time I'd been forced to see that I wasn't the only one struggling with feelings I couldn't control.

I wasn't the only one who felt like I was drowning.

From that day, I quit fighting at school and worked hard to be the best son I could be. I made a pact to never see my mother cry again. But she cried when she told me about the cancer.

That same night I took a walk and someone tried to take my wallet. Beating his ass made me feel better. Somehow that turned into nightly walks, where I'm looking for trouble. The worst part is that I don't know if I can stop. I've come to crave it, the violence, the release of my anger. It's the only thing that soothes me.

Except for Emma.

She's always so still and perfect, like a sculpture you're not supposed to touch. When she looks at me, something calms inside as if I'm at peace. I feel corny even thinking that so I focus on the road.

Two of my brothers, Gabriel and Zachary, run a bike repair shop in the neighboring city of West Haven. I park my bike out front and send an admiring glance at the Harley Night Rod directly in front of the door. I look up at the sign. G&Z Motors.

This is the place.

The bell over the door tinkles merrily as I enter the shop. The television in the reception area broadcasts some reality show about tattooing. A man straightens behind the counter. He has dark hair like mine. Dark eyes like mine.

"Can I help you?"

The name tag on his breast pocket reads *Gabe* but I know who he is before he even speaks. I was sure on the way here that this was the right move but now that he's standing in front of me, I'm not sure what to say.

He stares back at me staring at him for a full minute before he speaks. "You're one of them, aren't you?" he says finally.

I don't need to ask what he means. Tons of things were going through my mind on the way here but it hadn't occurred to me that he would look like me. But he does. Probably more so than Finn.

"Zack! Get out here." He yells over his shoulder, his deep voice barely carrying over the racket coming from the back of the shop. The noise doesn't stop.

"Give me a second." He disappears behind the wall and a few minutes later the noise stops. I wonder what he's saying to the other one. Zachary. This whole situation is so backwards. I wish briefly that I'd brought Finn with me. Then I realize that I can bring them with me later to meet him. Ambush him at the apartment since he seems so determined not to leave.

Gabe comes back out and another man follows. He looks slightly younger and the sides of his hair are shaved completely bald. There are tattoos running down each side of his skull. He stares back at me, taking in my height and worn T-shirt.

"That had to hurt like a bitch." I jerk my chin toward the tattoos on his head.

He looks surprised and then shrugs. "Life hurts."

A full grin takes over my face and I can tell he's not sure what to make of it. But with that one statement, I know I've made the right decision.

"You're definitely my brother."

He grunts but the tension bleeds out of his shoulders so he doesn't look like he's primed for a wrestling match anymore.

"Is there somewhere we can talk?"

Gabe jerks his head toward the back. "Yeah, in the shop. No customers back here."

I follow him behind the counter. He's dressed preppy in slacks and a white collared shirt. Zack is the exact opposite in faded jeans and stained T-shirt. The back of the shop is much cleaner than I was expecting. There's a car up on rails and a bike in some stage of being dismantled across from where Zack slumps in a metal chair.

"Are you working on this one?" I nod my head at the disassembled bike.

He nods but doesn't volunteer any additional information. I take a seat in the metal folding chair next to him.

"I'm not here to disrupt your lives or anything. I didn't even know you existed and I just had to know. Shit, I'm not even sure what I needed to know by coming here. But I wanted to see you."

Gabe crosses his arms. "Interesting. You felt more for us than our own father did."

"He didn't raise you? I thought—"

"You thought he left your mom for ours?" Gabe guesses. "No. Our moms were best friends and he almost broke up their friendship by sleeping with both of them. Neither of them knew what he was up to. He had them both convinced they were his girlfriend and that the other was just jealous. Luckily, they figured it out and they both kicked him to the curb. Not before realizing they were both pregnant though."

"Wow. That's pretty fucked up."

Zack snorts. "Tell me about it." When he doesn't look inclined to add anything else to the conversation, I look back to Gabe.

"So, you guys didn't grow up knowing each other then?"

"No, we did. Once he was out of their lives, our mom's renewed their friendship and they raised us together. They still joke that raising kids with your best girlfriend is a much better bet than raising them with a man. I honestly can't disagree. Zack's mom is like my second mother."

"This is all so crazy. I don't understand what he was doing. He ditched my mom when I was eight and Finn was five. Then he only came back briefly once. But now I realize, he must have come back after he'd already been with your moms. He was just a regular P.I.M.P. apparently."

They snicker and look at each other before turning back to me. "So, what do you *really* think old Max is up to?"

* * * * *

An hour later I park my bike in a space at the boardwalk. After spending time with my brothers, I'm in a good mood. There aren't too many people that I can talk to about my current fucked up situation. However, I'm determined to put it all out of my mind. It's a beautiful day, cool and crisp. The weather is unseasonably warm and I realize how close to spring we are.

The boardwalk isn't my favorite place, usually because it's chock full of tourists, but this is where Emma wanted to meet. I've asked her out for weeks so if she's willing to give me a chance, I'm willing to meet wherever she wants.

Emma stands a few spaces over peering into the trunk of an older sedan. When she straightens and sees me walking toward her, she waves. "Hey. I thought we could take a walk on the beach. I packed a small cooler for us."

She points to the small red and white cooler in the trunk of her car. I lift it easily.

"Did you pack anything for me?" It doesn't feel like there's much in the cooler and definitely not enough to feed two people.

She blushes. "Probably not enough." Her head disappears into the front seat of the car and when she emerges, she's holding a thick multicolored beach towel.

"I'm prepared."

She's so cute that I don't have the heart to tell her that half of my body will likely be hanging off that towel. We walk down and find a spot on the sand. There are only a few people out here. It will be a completely different scene once summer comes. She spreads the towel and I set the cooler on one end to hold it down. Emma sits on the other end facing me.

"Are you hungry?"

I squint up at the seagulls diving above us. They remind me of my conversation with Finn a few days ago. At least I could tell my brother that I finally made it to the beach.

"I could eat. That's true pretty much all of the time."

She laughs softly. "Yeah, I'll bet. Well, if you're good, I even have desserts in here." She pulls out sandwiches, small snack bags of chips and a plastic container of red velvet cake.

"You know, I've never been on a date where the girl planned everything. Will I get my balls back after this is all over?"

She looks up at me, and then lets out a little giggle. "Is it that threatening?"

"No, I'm just joking. Badly, obviously." I look down the sand to where a few other couples sit on towels, similarly enjoying the unseasonably warm weather. The sky is a crystalline blue dotted with fluffy white clouds that look like floating cotton balls. I close my eyes and let the breeze coming off the water flow over me. Above me, I can hear the cry and call of the seagulls.

"I've never really been a beach person."

Emma stops her fussing with the food. "Sorry, we can go if

you'd rather do something else. I just thought it would be a quiet place we could talk."

"No, this is nice. I find myself willing to make an exception for you. So, how long have you worked for Patrick?"

Her face falls slightly. "Just a few months. After my parents died, Mr. Stevens was the one who handled their estate. He's an old family friend. I think he just feels sorry for me, really."

"I'm so sorry. I didn't realize."

"No, it's okay. I know you didn't know."

We sit in awkward silence for a minute before she asks, "So, what about you. What did you do before you worked as a bodyguard?"

"I was in the military. I've been working for Alexander Security ever since I got out."

"What branch of the military?"

"Army."

She looks at me expectantly when I don't provide any additional details.

"Most of the missions I was on were classified so I can't really talk about them."

"Of course. I don't need to know details. I was just wondering what you did, you know, in general?"

"Um, I was a sniper actually."

"Oh. Really?" Her eyes go round and she takes a big bite of her sandwich.

I dig in the cooler looking for another sandwich. Anything to distract me from this painful silence. What am I supposed to say, I used to kill people? I did scary stuff that I hope you won't ever have to know about? There's just nothing that I can say to put her mind at ease. I'm reminded of my last girlfriend, Jenna's, words.

You're just too much sometimes, Tank. Too damn much to deal with.

"Oh. Well. Okay then." Her eyes roam over the sand, the waves crashing to the shore and then to the birds flying overhead. She's working as hard as I am to think of something to change the subject. Apparently she's not having any more luck than I am.

Damn this is awkward.

"Don't worry. That's always a conversation killer. It's not just you."

Her eyes light up. "Good. I mean, not good that it's a hard question to answer but good that … oh, never mind. So, tell me more about you. What's your family like?"

A smile tugs at the corners of my lips. "That shouldn't be a difficult question to answer either. And yet, it is. I apologize, Emma. This is the least normal date you've probably ever been on. To answer your question, I grew up with my younger brother, Finn. He's like a shorter, less attractive, version of me."

Her lips quirk up at the corners. "I'm sure. Sorry if it feels like I'm questioning you, or something. I didn't mean to pry."

"You weren't. You are asking perfectly normal questions. It's just that my life is a little too *reality show* for a girl like you to understand."

"What does that mean? A girl like me?" She raises her eyebrows.

"The kind of girl who grew up with two parents and a dog. The kind of girl who wears sweater sets and thinks *hell* is a bad word."

Her mouth falls open. "I have absolutely no idea what to even say to that."

I lean over and tuck a strand of her sunny hair behind her ear. The stuff is always sticking up all over the place and for some reason, I love it. Anyone else would look like an electrocuted poodle but on her, the effect is charming.

"Don't worry about it, buttercup. It's not an insult. We're just different, that's all."

She regards me from beneath lowered lashes, her gray eyes worried. Her teeth clamp down on her bottom lip. "What about your dad?"

"Uh, my parents divorced when I was a kid. So what did you do before you worked for Patrick?" Talking about my deadbeat dad is not the way to get this date back on track.

"I was in school. I was in my junior year when my parents died. Even though the school gave me a leave of absence to deal with everything, I couldn't keep my focus even after I came back. My grades suffered. I had a partial scholarship but you have to maintain a certain GPA to keep it. So now I'm trying to earn enough money to go back and retake some of the classes I failed."

"Makes sense. Is that why you started dancing at the Black Kitty?"

Her head snapped up. "Dancing? Oh god, you mean *stripping*? I'm not a stripper."

The disdain in her voice is obvious. I know she doesn't mean anything by it but after everything I've witnessed over the past twenty-four hours, it strikes me as incredibly ironic that most of the girls stripping at the Black Kitty are probably farther along in their college studies than she is. Most of them are dancing to pay their way through school. Or to support their kids.

"Are you okay?" Emma asks.

Part of me says to just write this whole thing off as a bust, to grab my shit and go home. But I'm so disappointed. So damn disappointed because I thought she was different. I contemplate not answering. She doesn't get it and people like her never do. But something inside me wants her to understand.

"Those girls you look down on are just doing what they need to survive. Half of them are in college and will probably make more money than either of us when they finish."

I shake my head but before I can say anything else my phone vibrates in my pocket. I pull it out. Normally I wouldn't take a phone call in the middle of a date, even one as spectacularly bad as this one but when I see my mom's name on the screen, I answer immediately.

"Hey, Mom. Is everything okay?"

"Hi baby. Yes, I'm fine. I just can't find my pills. I think I remember you setting them all out for me in that nifty little pill case. The one with the days of the week on it, right?"

"Yeah, I left it right on the kitchen island so you'll see it every morning."

"That's what I thought but it's not there."

I sit up on my knees and start placing things back in the cooler. Emma watches me and then starts packing up the items she took out.

"I'll come find it for you, Mom."

"Don't be silly. There's no need for you to drive out here just for that. I'm sure it'll turn up. I probably just moved it while I was cleaning off the counter and now I don't remember where I set it down. You know I do that sometimes."

It's been happening more and more lately. She's forgetting things and doing things that don't make sense. It worries me. What if she forgets she's already taken her medicine and then takes it again? She could overdose herself without even realizing it.

"I'm in Virginia Beach anyway. I'll be there in a minute."

After I hang up with my mom, I turn to Emma. "My mom can't find her medication. She does this sometimes. Misplaces things. I need to get over there. I'm sorry to bail on you."

She follows me, her legs working double time on the sand to keep up with my long strides. "It's no problem. I think it's nice that you're so devoted to your mom."

"Well, she did whatever she had to do to keep us all together when we were growing up. We didn't have a lot of money but she never let us down. Now it's our turn to take care of her."

When we reach the parking lot, I wait while she fumbles with the keys on her chain to find the right one. She opens the trunk so I can place the cooler inside.

"Sorry I have to cut things short." Even though things weren't going well, I still feel bad about running out on her. I've been hitting on her for weeks and now the first time she says yes, I ditch her after less than an hour.

"No, I understand completely. I hope your mom is okay." Emma closes the trunk and then unlocks the front door of the car. I wait while she slides behind the wheel.

"Thanks. I'm sure she's fine. I just want to check on her."

She turns the key and her engine strains to turn over. It sounds like it's pleading for help.

"Ugh, I hate this stupid car." She tries it again and a cloud of smoke erupts from beneath the hood. Emma gets out of the car and waves her hand in front of her face. "Maybe I shouldn't have said that. Now I've pissed her off."

I glance at my cell phone again. There's no way I have time to get beneath the hood and figure out what's wrong. But I also can't just leave her here alone. I could take her home and come back for her car later but that would be going completely out of the way. And my mom didn't sound good.

"Come on."

She leans in and grabs her bag from the passenger seat of her car. "I'm so sorry. You don't have to stay. I'll call Ivy. Or maybe Sasha can pick me up."

"What if they can't come right away?"

She places a hand over her eyes shielding them from the midday sun. "It's a beautiful day. I'll just hang out until they can get here."

I don't even have to think about it. Every instinct I have revolts at the idea of leaving her somewhere alone without a guaranteed way to get home. Normally I wouldn't take a girl home to meet my mom this soon. Or ever. But in this case, it really doesn't matter. We tried and it didn't work out. I'm not the only one feeling the awkward vibes so there's no way she wants to see me again either.

"Yeah, no. You're coming with me buttercup."

She wrinkles her nose at the nickname but follows me as I walk over to my bike.

"I really wish I hadn't worn a skirt now."

My lips curl up as I look at her slender legs peeking from beneath the billowy layers of her skirt. "I don't mind."

Her annoyed response is drowned out by the roar of the engine as I start the bike. She climbs on behind me and wraps her arms around my waist. "Where are we going anyway?"

I flip the visor down on my helmet before I answer. "I'm taking you home with me."

* * * * *

We walk up to the doorway of my mom's house and I hit the bell. Despite it being after lunchtime the curtains in the front are still drawn. After several minutes, I glance back at Emma. She's looking around curiously but doesn't seem impatient.

"It takes a little longer for her to get to the door these days. The chemo hits her pretty hard."

I'm not sure why I'm explaining anything to Emma. I chuckle a little under my breath. Men really do think with their dicks. Despite her snide comments on the beach, there's a part of me that's still hanging on to the idea of her. That date proved without a shadow of a doubt that my fascination with her is completely chemical. So I shouldn't care at all what she thinks about anything and I definitely shouldn't be sharing intimate details with her.

The door finally opens. Mom is wearing her oversized nightshirt and a pair of sweatpants. They hang off her. I make a mental note to buy her smaller sizes until she gains back some of the weight she's lost.

"Tank. I told you not to come. But since you're here, you can fix the television for me. Who is this?" Her eyes stop on Emma and she glances at me.

"Mom this is my friend, Emma. Emma, this is my mom, Claire Marshall."

"Sorry, I know I must look a mess." Mom pats the bandanna tied over her thinning hair self-consciously.

I should have anticipated this. But I'm a guy and we don't think about this kind of stuff. We don't worry about how our hair looks or what we're wearing. But I would never do anything to embarrass my mom.

I should have just dropped Emma off, gas mileage be damned.

"Sorry Mom for just dropping in on you with company. But I wanted to make sure that you were okay."

I don't say it out loud but she hadn't sounded too good on the phone. The lines around her eyes are more pronounced and she looks tired. Really tired. It's a scary thing to see her looking like this. It reminds me of why I've made the decisions I've made recently. It's all for her. She deserves everything Finn and I can give her.

"Come on in."

We walk past her and into the house. It's dark with the curtains drawn.

"Let me just change my clothes. And try to do something with this hair. It's so hard to wash my hair in the shower now. I get dizzy sometimes."

"I used to wash my sister's hair in the sink when we were younger," Emma comments.

"In the sink? That's a good idea." Mom pats the bandanna on her hair again.

"Do you want me to help?" Emma takes off her jacket and then rolls up her sleeves. "I was usually helping her strip out a bad dye job so a simple wash should be easy."

Mom looks shocked but then smiles at her. "Would you? I'd love it."

They walk toward the kitchen and I follow behind. "Do you guys need any help?"

Emma scrunches her nose up at me. "No boys allowed."

"I'll just go grab my shampoo and a towel." Mom leaves the kitchen, seeming more cheerful than I've seen her in weeks.

Emma curls a hand around my forearm. "Don't worry. She'll be sitting the whole time with her head over the sink. This way she doesn't have to worry about slipping in the shower. It'll be fine."

My mom keeps canned sodas in the back of the fridge for me so I pull out a cola and take it back to the living room. I flip on the television but keep the volume low in case they need me. The soft murmur of their voices and the occasional burst of laughter filter in from the kitchen but otherwise it's silent. It's a good silence. A peaceful silence. We haven't had much of that lately.

No matter what happened before on our date, Emma has given me the most unexpected gift. She's taken my mom's mind off the chemo and brought it back to the land of the living. She's smiling and laughing again just like she used to. There's nothing in the world that could mean more to me.

As Emma is cleaning up, my mom comes and sits on the couch next to me, rubbing her hair absently with the fluffy blue towel around her neck.

"I'd forgotten what it's like to just laugh and gossip about nothing. We put so much focus on treatments and therapies and we overlook the simplest joys. Laughter. This was a really nice day."

She glances over at me. There's a silly little smile on her face, one I haven't seen before.

"What?"

"Nothing. Just that I like her."

"It's not a big deal, Mom. She's just someone I'm helping out. A friend of a friend."

"Still, I like her." She watches me with her knowing eyes. "It's okay to like someone, Tank. Not everyone leaves. I know your father left. And now I'm … I'm leaving you." Her voice breaks a little and

I'm not sure I can listen to this.

"*Mom*," I warn, not wanting to hear anything else she has to say. Not if it's going to be talk about her leaving us.

"I'm just saying, it's okay to like someone."

"Okay, I'm not talking about girls with you. That's not happening. And you aren't going *anywhere*. I've got the money for your surgery."

Her hands fly to her mouth. "How could you have gotten that much money so fast?"

"I told you I've been working really hard and I just had to figure a few things out. Finn and I worked it out. We've got it covered now. I don't want you to worry about anything."

"You're keeping something from me. I know it. Just tell me that you didn't do anything illegal."

"Mama." The word takes me by surprise even as it leaves my mouth. I haven't called her that since I was a kid. "I told you, you don't have to worry. It's nothing like that. It's just Finn and I moving some money around. Okay?"

She doesn't speak but her shoulders sag a little as she sits back. "Good. Okay. I just worry about you, Tank. I worry about you most of all."

Chapter Seven

Emma

"You don't have to clean that up dear. I can do it." Claire stands in the doorway of the kitchen watching me with an amused look. She rubs her hair absently with a towel.

"I'm almost done. See?"

As I sponge up the puddles of water around the sink, I sneak glances at her. She looks so young to have a son Tank's age and she's a lot of fun. We spent a pleasurable hour while I was washing and conditioning her hair talking about my college classes and all the things she regrets doing during her college years. It shouldn't have taken that long really but I wasn't in any hurry and Claire didn't seem to be either.

She'd asked all kinds of questions. I think she's wondering what my relationship is to Tank.

"All done." I wring out the sponge and place it back on the counter. I already gathered up the loose hair in the sink and put the caps back on the shampoo and conditioner bottles. "I kind of wish we had time to do manicures and pedicures, too."

I try to remember the last time I had this much fun. It's been a long time since Ivy and I have done anything together. Everything these days is about money and our lack of it. She's always with Jon lately and I've been working around the clock. There's not a lot of time for laughter. I hadn't realized until now just how much I've missed it.

"I do, too. Visitors are few and far between these days. I tell you what, cancer lets you know who your real friends are. Mainly it's my boys." Claire presses another section of hair between the folds of the towel, blotting out the excess water. "They come out every few days to check on me and they call everyday. So I can't complain."

I lean back and observe Tank as he sits on the couch. There's so much that I want to ask her about him. Has he always been so intense? He seems to carry a heavy weight around with him. He helped me the other day and he didn't have to do that. Anyone else would have given me a ride home and then driven off without a care. Instead he took me home and put me in his bed. Which would have seemed self-serving except he didn't take advantage.

Even when I wanted him to.

Tank comes in the kitchen and places his empty soda can in the recycling bin. The trash can is almost full so he pulls the bag out and ties it off. "Let me take this out before we go." He opens the back door and takes the trash to the can directly outside the door.

"Okay, Mom. We should get going. I didn't mean to keep Emma out this long. I don't want her to get sick of me yet."

Claire holds out her arms and Tank enfolds her in a hug. "Thank you for coming darling. I really appreciate it."

To my surprise, Claire pulls me into a hug, too. "And you too, Emma. I'm sorry I interrupted your afternoon together. Well, not really since I had too much fun to be sorry. But you should take her out again, Tanner. Make it up to her."

"I'm not sure if that would be a reward or a punishment. Maybe she's had enough already." He squeezes her arm and she smiles up at him. It's so funny to watch Tank deal with his mother. He's so careful with her.

Claire walks us to the door.

"Lock up behind us, Mom." Tank waits until she closes the door and we hear the latch slide into place.

I follow him down the driveway to his bike. He hands me the helmet but I don't put it on.

"You're different than I was expecting. This whole day has been so different. I didn't even want to go but …"

"But what?"

"It's just you. The thing you said back at the beach. I've been thinking about it ever since. You're right. I was being judgmental.

You made me think about things, really think. I wouldn't have expected that from you. Most guys just look at women taking their clothes off as entertainment. Not as people."

He holds my gaze and then tugs on a lock of my hair. "It's not hard to see them as people if one of them is cutting the crusts off your peanut butter sandwiches and waking you for school in the morning."

Shame slams into me. "Tank, I'm sorry. I didn't know."

"I know. But I misjudged you, too. One thoughtless comment doesn't override the good things. You were really great with her. I haven't heard her laugh like that in a long time."

"Your mom is awesome. She told me about all the gorgeous men she dated in college."

He grimaces. "Yeah, she can be a little TMI with the details."

I laugh. "That was the best part. I listened shamelessly and made her tell me every detail. Twice."

He laughs along with me. "Good. Maybe she'll tell all that stuff to you and not to me or Finn."

"My mom had this salon she liked to go to and they would do her hair in the most beautiful styles. So, I never really had an at home spa day with her. Now I'm just left wondering how many other things we never got to do. How many other things did I miss out on because I thought we had plenty of time?"

The words dry up and I'm left staring back at him with this sick sense of despair that I can't express. My throat closes up and there's this awful burn behind my eyelids.

"I'm sorry about your mom, Emma. I would say I understand but I'm starting to realize that I don't have the slightest clue."

I grab his hand. It's huge and there are callouses on the palm. I rub my thumb over the rough skin while I gather my thoughts.

"Your mom is still here and you're doing exactly what you should be. Spending time with her. Appreciating her. And I don't know what's going on between you and your dad, but it's not too late to make up with him either."

I can tell he doesn't know how to respond. I'm probably annoying him, pushing my nose into his business. We barely know each other and I'm trying to tell him how to live his life? But in that moment what I'm saying has nothing to do with Max Marshall, his money or doing a job. It's one hundred percent truth and I like Tank enough to want to make sure he hears it.

"I know it's none of my business but I feel like I have to warn you. Need to make sure you understand. Your mother, your father can be taken from you at any time. And you never realize how lucky you are to have parents, until you don't."

"You're right. But my family situation … it's complicated."

I look back at the house where Claire stands in the window watching us. I hand the helmet back to Tank and walk back up the driveway. Before I even get to the door, Claire has it open. She's watching me with this patient expression. It's like she knows what I need and she's just waiting for me to figure it out.

I take the last few steps at a run, almost knocking her over with a hug. My shoulders shake uncontrollably as I try to rein in my emotions. When I'm finally composed again, she wipes the tears from my face and smiles at me.

"It was so wonderful meeting you, Emma. Tank had better bring you back to see me. And if he doesn't, be patient with him."

"I will. Thank you."

Tank is watching us with a baffled expression but he doesn't say anything as I get on the back of his bike. He puts the helmet on my head and secures the strap beneath my chin. He's so careful, like he's afraid to hurt me.

He's hard to resist on any given day but now, after seeing him with his mother, it's pretty much fact.

Tank Marshall is irresistible.

* * * * *

We pull up outside of the house. Ivy's car is the only one in the driveway. Jon loves taking her to fancy hotels, which she thinks is his way of showing her a good time. In my opinion it's pretty sketchy, like he can't take her to his house. Secretly, I think he's already got a girlfriend.

She texted me earlier that they wouldn't be back until tomorrow. It's only a temporary reprieve but I'll take it. I know I need to get my own place. They might be out now but eventually he'll end up back here. I don't want any repeats of the other morning.

"Is that his car?" Tank looks over his shoulder at me. He's so close that I can smell the scent of his leather jacket and the aftershave he uses. It's nice. Oh who am I kidding? It makes me want to climb inside his coat with him.

"No. They're not here."

"I hate the idea of leaving you here alone. What if he comes back?"

"He's not dangerous, Tank. Just annoying and gross. As long as Ivy's with him, he'll be in her room. I won't have to see him until morning. I'm going in to work early tomorrow anyway." I climb off the back of the bike and unstrap the helmet. My hair is stuck to my forehead so I run a hand through it trying to fluff it out a little.

"I'll pick you up."

"No, you don't have to do that."

"Your car is still back at the beach, remember?"

After spending the evening with his mom, I totally forgot about my car. The smoke coming from beneath the hood probably means my cracked radiator finally busted. The last time I got it serviced, they told me I needed a new one. I didn't have the money for it then and I still don't. I could probably ask Ivy to borrow some but I already know her solution to the problem. She'll ask Jon for the money and there is no way that I want to owe him anything. I'd rather walk.

"I might as well leave it there. I need a new radiator. And probably a new engine, too."

"I'll take care of it. After I'm done, I'll bring it back to you at work. No arguments. After all, you just spent the past hour helping my mom out. We're friends, right? It's no big deal to help a friend out."

I can't think of anything to say. He's making it easy for me to accept his help without feeling like a total charity case but it still feels like too much. "I can pay you back. At least for the parts."

He shakes his head. "You can make me dinner."

"You drive a hard bargain. I'll make you dinner if we eat at your mom's house."

He looks at me in surprise.

"What? I really had fun today. Plus, I can tell she really enjoys it when you visit. So I'll cook there if you don't think she'll mind."

"No, she'll love it. We haven't had many family dinners lately. First because she wasn't feeling well and then Finn, well, my brother doesn't go out much now. Do you mind if I invite him?"

"Of course not. I think your mom will be really happy to have both of you there. What's he like? Your brother, I mean."

He glances at me and his lips tighten. "Never mind. I'm definitely not inviting him. He'll spend the entire night hitting on you and then I'll have to pound my own brother."

Heat spreads through me at his possessive statement. After our disastrous beach date, I figured he wasn't interested anymore. I definitely wouldn't have expected him to be jealous at the idea of his brother hitting on me. Why would he even care?

"I'm sure he won't even notice me. Ivy's the one who has men panting after her everywhere she goes."

His gaze holds mine. "You have men panting. If you don't know that, then you aren't paying attention."

I suck in a breath as his breath washes over my face. His eyes drop to my lips as he gets closer. Is he going to kiss me now? I lick my lips and his eyes immediately go to my mouth. Then he leans closer and grabs the helmet from my hands. He sits back, looking all together too satisfied considering that he's gotten me all riled up. Then it dawns on me that he's playing with me.

I adjust my bag and start walking up the driveway. When I turn around, he's still watching me with a small smile.

"What?"

That smug smile gets even wider. "Nothing. I told you I'd get you to dinner one of these days."

Then he starts the engine, drowning out any reply I would have made, and pulls off leaving me staring after him.

* * * * *

The next day, I'm completely distracted. Even Mr. Stevens notices when I call one of his longtime clients by the wrong name. Luckily we're so busy today that I don't have time to brood. Tank called this morning and offered me a ride to work but luckily Ivy was home. Seeing him first thing in the morning would have been too much. I need time to think without him there clouding my mind.

I only get out of the office to pick up a deli sandwich for Mr. Stevens. I don't eat my own lunch until after three o'clock, a ham and cheese sandwich I threw together on the way out the door this morning.

When I take a bite, I discover that I didn't put any mustard on the bread. I let out a disgusted sigh.

"I know that sound. Dating trouble?" Mr. Stevens puts a file on my desk and then leans against the wall.

"Not really. We're not really dating." I glance at him from the corner of my eye. He looks like a lawyer with his standard blue suit, red tie and strong jaw line. If his brown hair wasn't thinning in the front, he'd look like an actor playing a lawyer on a crime drama. He's always come across as logical, objective and fair. He's the perfect person to ask for an impartial opinion about Tank. As far as I know, they don't know each other outside of their professional relationship.

"It's about Tank Marshall. I went on a date with him. And it was nice. Strange but nice. But I don't have a lot of experience dating. You've been working with him for a while now. Does he come across as a decent guy to you?"

Patrick looks uneasy. "Look, kiddo. I can't divulge information about my clients. You know that. But that family … just watch yourself, Emma. You've had a rough year and I don't want to see you get hurt."

"Of course. Thanks, Mr. Stevens."

He nods and then disappears back into his office. *Well, that tells me absolutely nothing.* Since Patrick can't tell me anything and I have nothing else to go on, I'll have to use my own judgment here. What's the big deal? I'm just supposed to be friendly to the guy and then put in a good word for his dad. I shouldn't have to know his entire background to do that. But as I pack my things to leave for the day, I know I'm just fooling myself. I want to know more about Tank for reasons that have nothing to do with Maxwell Marshall or his insane job offer.

I want to know him because I'm attracted to him. Which is the number one reason I need to stay far away.

As if my thoughts have conjured him, Tank comes through the door at five minutes before closing time. He's wearing the same beat-up leather jacket he had on a few nights ago at the club. His dark hair is spiked up at the top but not in a *metrosexual I use hair product* kind of way. This looks more like he's growing out a buzz cut and his hair hasn't figured out which direction is down yet.

"You don't have an appointment today."

He acknowledges the observation with a slight nod. "I don't. I didn't need all those other appointments either. But I'm sure you've figured that out by now."

A warm tendril of pleasure unfurls inside me at his words. The thought had crossed my mind because he seemed to have more frequent appointments than any of our other clients but to hear him confirm it out loud is unexpected. He's so ... *forward*, sometimes. It's like he has no fear, of rejection or embarrassment. Then again, considering the things he told me yesterday on our beach date, he's had far worse to deal with in his life than a girl hurting his feelings.

"Maybe. But then maybe you flirt with every girl you meet."

"No. I do a lot of things with you that I don't do with anyone else."

"Oh, you aren't normally a beach-going kind of guy?" I tease. He'd seemed so out of place at the beach, like he wasn't quite sure how to relax.

"Or an *ask a girl out repeatedly* kind of guy. I just don't care that much as a general rule." He tucks his hands in his pockets. "You seem to be the exception."

"Lucky me." I gather my things and then slide my arms into my coat. He follows behind me as I walk out of the law office. My car is parked directly in front of the door.

"You fixed it already?" I'd spent so much time obsessing over Tank that my car had completely slipped my mind.

"It turns out, I know a guy." He laughs softly and I figure there's probably way more to that story than I know.

"Still, thank you. If I'd had to go to my usual garage it would have taken at least a week before they'd finished with it. And they'd want my life savings and the blood of my future firstborn child." I pull out my phone to text Ivy that I don't need a ride anymore.

"No sacrificial lamb will be needed this time. Although, I feel bad about how off-track things got yesterday. We were interrupted, and then you end up playing hairdresser for my Mom and cleaning her kitchen. This can't stay on my record. I need a do-over."

"Well, the thing is I'm not going home. Today is my day to volunteer at the animal shelter."

Tank leans closer and my breath seizes in my throat when he tucks a strand of hair behind my ear. He's so close that I can see that his eyes are actually a mixture of brown and green.

"Can't you skip today? I really want to spend some time with you, Emma."

Something clenches deep and low in my belly as his fingers

brush over my cheek. I *could* skip going to the shelter but I know they really count on my help. They can't afford to hire more people due to budget cuts. Blowing it off just to go out with a guy, a guy that I'm not even sure I really like, seems pretty crappy. A hot guy should not trump poor, sweet helpless animals. Although my libido doesn't seem to agree. There is a completely shameless hussy inside of me that doesn't care at all about the helpless strays at the shelter. I shake my head and open the driver's side door of my car.

"I can't. They really need all the help they can get. But wait, you could come with me. We could use the extra set of hands." I smile pleadingly, hoping that he'll come. Lusting after him isn't so bad if he's using those muscles to help out charity, right?

"I'm not really an animal person."

"How can you not be an animal person? Animals give love so freely and they don't hurt anyone. Not like people. Come on. This can be our do-over. What do you say?" I find myself holding my breath waiting for his answer.

I want this do-over just as much as he appears to. I can't ask him more about his relationship with Mr. Marshall without making him defensive. But maybe I can find out how he feels about the rest of his family. Maybe that will give me a clue as to why he's so against the idea of reconciling with his dad.

"Okay, you've convinced me." Tank walks around the car and gets in the passenger seat. "There won't be any interruptions this time."

Chapter Eight

Tank

"So where is this place we're going?" I'm prepared for the next hour or so to be pure torture. But if dealing with a bunch of pitiful creatures makes Emma more likely to give me another chance then I'll do it.

"Near the community college. Back when I was in school, one of the guys in my biology class, Brett, mentioned that they needed volunteers. He's studying to be a veterinarian, too. If I hadn't had to drop out, we'd probably be in vet school together."

"Everyone's life takes a different path. I'm not sure why. Hell, I have absolutely no answers. But your path isn't wrong, Emma. It's yours and you'll make it meaningful and right. Don't compare yourself to others."

"You're completely right. I just need a reminder of that some days." Emma smiles over at me before turning into the parking lot in front of a small white building.

"The owner, Dr. Kenya Marsh, is really appreciative of all volunteers. This place is exactly what I want to do after I finish school. I want to offer veterinarian services to people who can't afford it. Dr. Marsh has an open clinic one Saturday per month so that everyone can make sure their animals get preventative care."

We climb out of the car and I follow her into the white building. Emma bypasses the front desk and walks down the hall. I follow since she seems to know where she's going. We enter a room in the back, filled with metal cages. It smells like pee.

Christ, I must really like this girl.

"Hi Brett. How are the babies, today?" Emma asks as she shrugs out of her coat. She hangs it on a peg behind the door so I do the same.

A young man with dark, tightly curled hair turns around. In his arms are two black and white kittens. "Great, I'm just getting some playtime in with Thing 1 and Thing 2."

Emma accepts one of the kittens and holds it gently in her palms. "Hello, Uno. Did you miss me? I missed you."

Brett shakes his head. "She can always tell them apart. I don't know how she does that."

I watch in amazement as Emma lights up. How wrong I was to

think that she never smiles. Obviously I'm just not the right audience. She is wearing the biggest, most beautiful smile right now. When she turns to me, her face bent so she can rub her cheek against the kitten's soft fur, my heart gives an extra thump.

"You are so beautiful."

"Huh? Did you say something, Tank?

"Uh, they're beautiful. The kittens."

She smiles her agreement and then sits right on the floor and allows the kittens to crawl all over her lap. Brett moves around the room, opening a few other crates and taking out their occupants. Before long the room is a meowing, hissing, purring cacophony of sound.

"Most of the cats don't get a lot of one-on-one affection. That's where we come in. I do some chores to help Brett take care of them but also I get to play with them." She hands me a calico kitten nicknamed "Patches."

"Wait, what am I supposed to do?" A tickle of panic threatens. I've never had a pet. My mom could barely afford to feed us, let alone an animal.

"Just give them some love. I'm going to help Brett clean out a few cages."

Give them some love. Right. Like I know what that means.

Emma moves away, chatting easily with Brett. The other man squeezes her arm, his touch lingering a bit longer than necessary. I look down at the calico kitten currently trying to climb the front of my T-shirt.

"This is not going the way I'd hoped, cat. I'm supposed to be charming her, convincing her to give me a chance and now she's off with that guy and I'm stuck here with you."

Patches meows plaintively.

"It sounds like you agree." I run a finger experimentally over the kitten's soft little head. It stretches into the caress. It's so small it almost looks like a toy. It fits in the palm of my hand. There's a movement to my right so I turn to see what it is and then immediately jerk backward. A hairless thing stands at my elbow, watching me with narrowed eyes.

"Uh, Emma. What is that?"

She turns to see what I'm talking about. "Oh, that's Poochie."

"What's a poochie? And why is it bald?" The thing blinks at me with huge golden eyes. Now that I'm not so startled it looks less threatening. It's so ugly it's almost cute.

"No, that's her name silly. She's a cat. A breed called a Sphynx. She's supposed to be hairless. Unfortunately, her last owner decided she wasn't cuddly enough and abandoned her outside in the middle of winter. I can't believe they just left her like that."

I look back at the cat, now watching me with strangely human eyes. An image comes back to me, watching my dad's car drive away from the house while my mom sobbed in the background.

"I think I know how she feels." I stretch out my hand, slowly, tentatively. Poochie's ears flicker but she doesn't move.

"Oh dude, she never lets anyone pet her. She's bitten me like five times." Brett stops when Poochie walks forward, her head bent, and allows me to stroke the top of her head.

"Well, I'll be damned. That mean ass cat finally took a liking to somebody."

"Tank, can you help me? This one is stuck." Emma points at one of the cages.

I stand carefully and Poochie retreats to the corner of the room. For the next hour, I help Emma and Brett by lifting cages and cleaning. It's an easy hour, surprisingly. One where I'm not required to think about myself, just what I can do to help out. I'm starting to understand what Emma meant earlier about animals not requiring anything from you other than love. I scratch the kitten Emma's holding behind the ears. Brett replaces the food and water in the cage we've just cleaned out.

I sit back down on the floor and Poochie slinks over. I'm not sure exactly what to do but she doesn't require me to do anything. She rubs up against my shirt using me as a makeshift rubbing post. Another kitten crawling on the floor nearby climbs into my lap and curls up.

"This is amazing. I'm still in awe. You're some kind of cat whisperer." Brett holds out a clipboard. "If you wanted to adopt her, it's easy. You fill out this form and then just pay the fees. She's already up to date on all her shots and stuff."

I'm shaking my head before he's even done with his spiel. "Adopt? I can't even keep a plant alive."

He looks over at Emma. "So, how are you two friends? It seems like a bit of an odd matchup."

I can't disagree with him but the way he's looking at her makes me want to stake my claim anyway. "Opposites attract, right? Besides, I'm sure Emma knows enough about animals for the both of us. I'm just here to help her out."

I stand up and place the kitten back in its crate. Emma appears at my elbow. "She's so cute."

While I'm not an animal lover the way she is, it would take a heart of stone not to be moved by some of these little balls of fluff.

Poochie follows us as we move around the room.

"Come on, cat. It's time to go." I try to coax her back to me but she seems to sense it's a trick. She gives me a mournful look and then retreats to the other side of the room. She presses herself against the wall, looking like she'd rather disappear than get back in the crate.

"She's not coming. Not that I blame her."

Emma makes a soft cooing sound. Poochie's ears twitch but she doesn't come any closer.

Brett waves a hand. "It's okay. You can go. Once you leave, I'll put her back. Thanks for the help today."

"Of course. See you next week, Brett. Good luck with your exam." She gives him a quick hug and then retrieves our coats. He watches her movements a little too closely for my taste. I grit my teeth and then shrug into my leather jacket.

There's a mournful cry from across the room. It's eerie, like the sound of a wailing ghost. Poochie yowls again when I step out of the room.

Emma doesn't move. She looks horrified. "Aw, Tank. She's

upset that you're leaving. Look at her."

Against my better judgment, I poke my head back in the room and look at the meddlesome cat. She's still doing that horrendous howling and trying to kamikaze dive against the wall.

"Okay, okay. Come here." I crouch down and she immediately comes to me. I scratch behind her ears and she emits a rumbling purr. Brett walks up behind us. Poochie opens one eye and hisses at him.

"Good girl," I mutter under my breath.

I stand again and Poochie rubs against my leg.

"Wow, I've never seen her take to anyone like this." Brett sounds amazed.

Emma looks up at me, her gray eyes soft. "She obviously has very high standards."

Before I know what I'm doing, I grab the clipboard. "This is a bad idea."

* * * * *

It takes a little while to complete the paperwork, pay the fees and then get Poochie into the car. Every few moments, I stop and look over at the cat in question. She looks like someone's wrinkled grandfather. I have no idea what the hell I was thinking when I started this but it's too late to back down now.

We stop at the store so I can purchase a cat carrier, food, bowls and a collar. Emma stays in the car while I navigate the pet supply aisle on my own. After I spend more money on cat crap than I've spent on myself in a while, I carry the bags back to the car. It takes a minute to coax Poochie over so I can put her in the carrier but she finally gives in. Then I slide back into the passenger side seat.

Emma starts the car. “Thank you for your help today. I know that wasn’t what you were expecting when you came to see me earlier.”

“I had fun.” Shockingly, I’m telling the truth. I enjoyed the experience far more than I’d expected to. I look into the backseat. The cat carrier is made partially of mesh so I can see Poochie in there leaning against the walls of the carrier.

“I even got an attack cat out of the deal.”

A wide grin stretches across her face. “Clearly you got the best end of this bargain.” She glances over at me. “So what now? I can take you home or you could come over for a while. No one is even home.”

There’s a soft invitation in her eyes. She’s never seemed particularly open to spending this much time with me. Spending time with the cats must have softened her up a bit.

“Sure. I can come over.”

All I know is that I’m not ready to go home yet. Being around Emma brings me the most profound peace. Everything inside me seems to settle down into an uncomplicated stillness. I’m not ready to let go of that just yet.

Emma pulls up to her house and turns off the car, leaving us in silence. Lightning streaks across the sky and she jumps. “Okay, we need to get inside the house.”

“You don’t like storms.”

She shakes her head. “I like them best when I’m safe, warm and dry inside.”

Emma climbs out of the car and then leans into the backseat to grab the cat carrier. She’s talking to the cat, telling her where we are and where we’re going.

I follow her up the walkway and wait while she wrestles with the door. There is a sudden boom of thunder that sounds extremely close. Then the skies open up and the rain falls in heavy sheets, the wind splattering the rain in an angry gush across the porch. Emma curses as we’re both instantly drenched.

“Finally,” Emma announces as the key slides into the lock. We stumble across the threshold in a wet heap. Our legs tangle together and I have to twist myself so that when we fall, I take the brunt of the force.

“I’m really glad I didn’t go to your place first, otherwise I would have been driving home in this!”

She pushes up from my chest but goes still when she ends up half-straddling me. There’s no way she’s missing the unmistakable press of my erection beneath her. Her gaze lifts to mine and her cheeks flush pink. But she doesn’t move.

We stay just like that, lost in each other’s eyes until another boom of thunder rends the air, breaking the spell.

I set her to the side gently and stand up. “Well, I’ve never had to go to such lengths to get a woman on top of me before.” She laughs and takes the hand I extend to her and pulls herself up.

She looks out the open door at the storm. “I thought it wasn’t supposed to rain until later tonight."

I didn't either but I can't say I'm upset about the forecast. I shrug out of my wet jacket and hang it on one of the metal hooks by the door. I toe out of my soggy shoes as well.

"Looks like you're stuck with me for a while."

Emma

Crap, crap, crap. What the hell am I supposed to do with Tank Marshall in my house?

After giving Tank a towel and pointing him in the direction of the bathroom, I flit around the living room, picking up stray items of clothing and fluffing the pillows on the couch. I glance over my shoulder nervously awaiting the moment he'll appear.

After depositing my armful of junk in the hall closet, I race back to the kitchen. Poochie is still crouching in her carrier, watching me move around the room with her golden eyes. I unzip the carrier so she can come out when she wants to but she doesn't seem interested in venturing any further just yet.

When I hear the telltale squeak of the bathroom door opening down the hall, I lean casually against the counter. Tank rounds the corner and I have to struggle to hold in a sigh of appreciation. He's cuffed his pants and removed his sweater, revealing a simple white shirt. It's tight enough to show the definition of his arms and shoulders. The muscles hinted at under his leather jacket are on full display now.

I force my eyes away from his chest and focus on the wall behind him. "Do you want some coffee or tea or something? I could put on a pot."

He runs his hands through his hair, the dark strands standing on end. "A cup of tea is fine. As long as it's no trouble."

I take a mug down from the cupboard and fill it with water at the sink. I'm all too aware of Tank watching as I move around the small kitchen. His gaze sears into my back and I have to fight the urge to yank my shirt down to cover my bottom.

Just as I'm about to put the cup in the microwave, the lights flicker. We both look up at the light fixture above us. *Please tell me this is not happening.*

The lights flicker again and a second later we're plunged into darkness.

"Emma?" Tank's voice comes from my left.

"I'm here. Don't worry, this happens during every storm. The lights will come back in a second." I put a hand out in front of me tentatively, walking forward slowly until I touch a hard surface. The counter. I place the cup of water down carefully.

I tap my foot impatiently, willing the electricity to come back. Usually when the lights go out it's only for a few minutes. It's strange standing here in the darkness but I'm not going to complain. The last time the power went out I was in the shower. This is a breeze compared to being in the dark while wet and naked.

A series of clicks sounds somewhere to my left before a small flame appears, floating disembodied in the dark. A moment later another flame appears, then another. Tank has obviously found the small lighter and candles I keep near the window for just this purpose.

In the light of the candles I can see him standing next to the window. He flips the small lighter closed and leans against the wall, staring out at the rain. In profile, he looks almost regal.

"This is surprisingly relaxing," he murmurs.

"Yeah it is." I clear my throat and looked away from the temptation that is Tank. The universe seems to be conspiring against me, determined to throw us together until I lose all resolve. Between ignoring him at the law office, and now being stranded together in the dark, part of me wants to just give in, rip my panties off and let the universe have the last laugh. But I'm not a femme fatale and seducing a man isn't something you can study in school.

Sasha taught me to dress up to play a part. At the Black Kitty, it was all about the costume. The illusion. But I don't want illusions and I don't want a fantasy. No one can teach me how to be sexy in real life. I'm woefully out of my element.

"Well, I suppose I can't offer you anything to warm you up. Unless you want a real drink." I gesture to the row of liquor bottles lined up on a sideboard against the wall. I still have brandy and scotch. They were my father's and the bottles haven't been touched since he died. The thought darkens my mood. I really should get rid of those. I'm not much of a drinker but occasionally like a glass of something when I curl up reading. Or when I've had a hell of a day.

"Brandy would be good. Only if you join me though." He looks at me, his dark eyes intense. "It's not good to drink alone. So they say anyway."

His eyes follow me as I walk to the sideboard and select a bottle. "One day I would really like to know who 'they' are. For people who don't exist they seem to have a lot of influence."

His soft chuckle rumbles through me as I pick up the bottle of brandy and stack two glasses together. I carry them over to the table and pour a small portion in each glass. In the dark the beauty of the storm is revealed, the rain and lightning putting on a private show of water and light. I take a sip of the brandy, enjoying the way it warms on my tongue.

"I haven't done this in ages." I sit in one of the wooden chairs by the window. "I used to love watching the rain. Whenever there was a storm my parents used to cut off all the lights and we'd all pretend we were camping out in the living room."

He sat in the chair across from me. He leaned over and took one of my hands. "You miss them." It was said as a statement.

"Yeah, I do." Just that quickly, I'm back there, hiding in the closet, terrified. I look up to see Tank watching me. "They were murdered. It was a home invasion."

His hand tightens around mine. "I'm so sorry, Emma. When you said they died ..."

"Most people assume it was a car accident. I usually don't correct the assumption. It's just easier that way but somehow with you, I don't know. It feels like you'd understand." I take my hand back and tuck it in my lap.

Touching him is becoming too easy, a habit I can't afford to adopt. But he's watching me with eyes that seem to reflect the kind of horror that I feel inside. He has the eyes of someone who has seen terrible things and survived. Maybe that's how I knew I could tell him. Somehow I knew he wouldn't make me talk about it. Instead he does exactly what I need him to do. Listen and be there.

"So what about you? Did you and Finn grow up around here, too?" I take another sip of brandy feigning calm. I'm way too interested in his story.

"Yeah, we were raised in Norfolk. Mom tried her best to do it all but she could only do so much." He sits back and folds his hands behind his head. "I just found out I have three half-brothers, too. My dad was busy after he left us. I didn't even know they existed until recently."

Everything he's saying sounds so foreign from the Maxwell Marshall that I know. How could he not have even known his brothers? Did something happen and they lost contact? It just doesn't sound right.

"Wow. I can't even imagine not knowing my sister."

He coughed and kept his eyes on the storm. "It sucks but that's life. I'm over it." Lightning streaks across the sky again and he's illuminated in the sudden flash of light. He looks tense despite his relaxed pose, the lines around his eyes and mouth more prominent.

I turn away and looked out at the rain. It seems unfair to watch him in such an unguarded moment, like catching him with his clothes off. Tank Marshall naked in any sense is not something I can handle right now.

I reach for the bottle of brandy on the table and pour a little more in my glass. I usually don't drink hard liquor but under the circumstances I don't think it would hurt to have seconds. If I'm going to be stranded in the dark with Tank, I need a little liquid courage.

I hold up the bottle and Tank nods. He holds out his glass for more. Even being careful, a little of the dark liquid splashes out onto his hand. He lifts his hand to his mouth and licks up the drops. I can't look away, the sight of his tongue sliding over his skin igniting a million different fantasies.

"See something you like?" His brown eyes soften as he watches me, his eyes lingering on my mouth.

I flush, the heat in my cheeks going straight between my thighs. It's bad enough to have these fantasies about him. It's unbearable for him to know about it. A man like Tank can have any woman he wants and no doubt has plenty, probably more than one at a time. I'm a goody two shoes, former Honor Society president who had only one boyfriend until college. Not exactly a good match.

"Like I was saying, you're just not what I expected. You seem, more normal than I would have thought."

He leans closer until our shoulders are almost touching. "You thought I was an arrogant meathead."

"You are arrogant. It would take a sledgehammer to chip

through that ego of yours."

"I'm confident. There's a difference." He shrugs and smiles, a slow easy grin that makes my heart bang an extra beat in my chest. "It's not my fault I'm always right."

"Modest, too."

He winks sending a tingle of awareness down my spine. "You're not exactly as you first appear either." He reaches over and takes the drink from my hand, setting it carefully on the table behind us.

"You're always so prim and proper but your hair tells the real story. It's wild and untamed. You try to control it with these grandma hairstyles but it doesn't work. This is goddess hair." His hands thread through my strands, tugging until the band restraining the thick locks falls away. My hair falls in a damp golden mass around my shoulders, a tangle of waves spilling into his hands.

"And these plain clothes." He pops the first button on my shirt free revealing the lace at the top of my bra. I suck in a hard breath at the sudden look of stark need on his face. His eyes are fixated on the gap in my shirt. The rise and fall of my chest makes my breasts strain against the confines of my bra. I put a shaky hand over my heart and rub my breastbone. It feels like I can barely breathe.

"But that's not who you are, is it? There's so much more inside of you. I can almost see it there beneath the surface, like the first embers of a fire that could rage out of control at any moment." He leans closer until he's directly in front of me, his big body between my legs completely invading my space. His scent curls around me, a rich heady aroma mingled with the crisp scent of rain.

I whimper softly as his fingers thread through my hair, skimming over my scalp and awakening a myriad of sensations. My head falls back, vulnerable and open to the soft probing lips that trail over my face and neck. He nips at the delicate skin right below my ear, licking and biting all the way down to the base of my throat.

"Open for me love. That's it." He lets out a soft growl when my mouth falls open on a pant. He takes advantage, his tongue dipping into my mouth. I love the invasion as he takes control. I can feel him all over.

I grip his arms, my nails digging into his biceps, caught between pushing him away and pulling him closer. He feels just like a man should, his firm muscles flexing beneath my fingers. And he's so strong. I take shameless delight in his obvious strength as he sits back and pulls me on his lap. I take the opportunity to run my hands all over his broad shoulders and over the hard muscles in his chest.

I press forward rubbing against his chest. The friction is delicious, and every time my nipples brush against his chest, something clenches deep. He's hot and hard beneath me and I can feel the stiff length behind his zipper. I want him inside, on top and all over me. I want to lose myself in him.

He pushes my skirt up, his fingers running up the insides of my thighs. I moan out loud when he presses his thumbs against my heat. Even through my panties, surely he can feel how wet I am already. Then his thumbs slip past the cotton barrier and brush over my naked sex. I shudder at the touch. It suddenly feels like I'm aching between my legs. And empty. So empty.

With that thought, I launch myself over his chest, fusing my mouth to his. He falls back with a soft grunt, wrapping his arms around me to keep us upright. A second later he has me under him, his hard body sliding in the cradle of my legs. His weight is a welcome distraction, all that delicious muscle on top of me. He kisses me like he can't get enough of my taste, licking and biting and sucking. I'm helpless to stop it even if I'd wanted to.

He holds me captive with his hands in my hair, his mouth insistent as he explores my lips, neck and throat. I'm suddenly not sure how we've gotten to this point, when we stopped talking and started kissing. I'm not even sure if I'll regret this in a few hours.

Oh my god, this is happening so fast.

My logical mind tries to intervene but is quickly overridden by the exquisite sensations racing through me. I grip his shoulders and push back some, trying to put a little distance between us. I can't think when we're wrapped around each other.

His gaze drops to my mouth again and he licks his lips, like he's remembering my taste and missing it already. I groan. Everything about him calls to me, his broad shoulders, his nimble fingers, his tormenting mouth and most of all, his knowing eyes.

I want him, whether it's a mistake or not. And all the logic in the world can't stop this.

* * * * *

Standing in the middle of my room, some of my reason comes

back. Tank followed me down the hall and now reclines on my bed, his arms folded behind his head. The silence is a little unnerving. I think he's waiting for me to change my mind.

But that's not what I want.

The past eight months of my life have been like walking through fog. I have panic attacks at the simplest things and constant uncertainty over what I should do, where I should go and what the future holds. But right here, right now, I'm not uncertain and I'm definitely not afraid.

I'm alive. Only Tank makes me feel this way.

"Come here," he whispers.

From anyone else the order would annoy me but from him, yeah I'll come anywhere he wants me to. I crawl across the bed, newly aware of how my body moves. His eyes follow every movement, taking in the arch in my back, the placement of my hand between his legs and then my thighs as I straddle him. When he looks up at me, his eyes are hooded. I'm slammed with a sharp ache deep in my belly at the raw, carnal desire in that look. He sees something he wants.

And it's me.

"You are so beautiful. So perfect." His hands skim over the skin of my arm and up into my hair. He always seems fixated on my hair. Now he's gripping it, twisting the long strands around his fist. I whimper, taken off guard by how hot it is to have him holding me like this. He's turned my hair into some kind of leash and the idea of him taking control that way is … startlingly arousing.

He pulls me forward and leans up at the same time until our

mouths meet again. I can't think with his mouth on mine. Suddenly, he turns us over, so I'm on the bottom and the weight of him settling on top of me is so good that I groan out loud. His jeans rub right up against my panties causing the fabric to slip and slide through the folds of my sex. My head falls back and I grind against him shamelessly. Every rock of his hips brushes against my clit and it's got me right on the edge. My skirt is around my waist at this point and when he looks down, he can see the white cotton and the wetness on the inside of my thighs.

"Look how wet you are for me. For this." He hooks a finger in the panties and pulls them to the side. Then his finger slides deep, pushing through my clenching muscles all the way up to his knuckle.

"Tank. I need…"

He bites my bottom lip and his eyes fix on mine, hot and hard. "I know what you need. You need this," his finger plunges deep again, "and you need me."

He pulls away briefly to yank his shirt over his head and push his jeans down. I take the opportunity to shed my shirt and wiggle out of my skirt. When I look over at him again, he's completely naked. As I watch, he rolls a condom over his thick shaft, his eyes holding mine the whole time. My breath leaves my lungs on a helpless sigh. His cock curves up, long and thick almost to his belly button. It's built on a large scale just like the rest of him.

"Wow. You're big everywhere, huh?" There's nothing but pure feminine appreciation in my voice.

He leans over me and whispers in my ear. *"And you're going to take every inch."*

I shiver at the erotic promise in those words.

When he climbs back on the bed, he settles himself between my legs and this time, there's nothing to shield me from the heat and hardness. It feels amazing, being surrounded by him.

Then he does something with his hips that nudges his cock right where I need him. My toes curl and my fingers grab helplessly at the sheets. His eyes don't leave mine as he flexes his hips again, this time thrusting deep.

"*Fuck*, Emma. You feel so good. So tight and wet."

His big body presses me into the mattress so I can barely move. All I can do is grip his shoulders, my nails digging into the muscles as I'm forced to accept what he gives me. His eyes are on mine the whole time, watching my every reaction, my every whimper, my every shudder as he takes me with long, forceful strokes.

I can't speak. I can barely even keep my eyes open when he's looking at me like this. It's too much. Too much sensation and too much intimacy. My muscles grip him tightly as he thrusts again, then once more. He's so deep, so incredibly deep that I know I'll be feeling him all day tomorrow and maybe the day after that. He's doing more than just making love to me, he's *branding* me.

The savage intensity in his eyes as he drills into me sends me over the edge.

I scream when I come. I can't hold back the sound as my orgasm tears through me, splitting me apart. Pleasure explodes, radiating out from where he's buried deep within me and all the way down to my toes.

As I clench around him helplessly, shaking with the last tremors of my orgasm, he hooks his hands beneath my knees and pushes them back toward my shoulders. The position spreads my legs and forces my pussy to open up to him, drawing him even deeper.

His mouth settles near my ear and the things he's saying as he thrusts into me, *oh god*, the things he's whispering to me. He tells me how warm and soft my pussy is, how tight it is, how wet it is. No one has ever talked to me like this and I'm melting, just disintegrating as he mindfucks me in a way that I've never experienced.

His deep growl of satisfaction as he comes pushes me even further away from sanity. It sounds animalistic, primitive.

Then again there's nothing civilized about Tank Marshall. And there never will be.

Chapter Nine

Emma

The following evening, I stand in the kitchen at Claire's house stirring a pot of spaghetti sauce. Tank stands next to me awkwardly chopping onions. So far this has been an incredibly strange Saturday afternoon. I wish I could say I was all modern and sleeping with a guy is no big deal but I'm completely unsure how to act around him now.

He left before Ivy and Jon came home so at least I didn't have to deal with any questions from my extremely nosy sister. Or any disgusting comments from Jon. I'd almost forgotten about our dinner plans until he called me up this afternoon. Once he found out that I hadn't gone grocery shopping yet, he insisted on picking me up. I've never been to the grocery store with a guy before. It was a completely new experience.

I had a list of exactly what I needed but Tank wanted to go up and down every aisle. I now know things about him that I would have never suspected. He has a sweet tooth but not for chocolate. Instead he likes raspberry flavored *everything*. Brand names were scrutinized and put back in favor of comparable store brands. I wouldn't have guessed that he would be a thrifty shopper. He also insisted on buying everything.

The doorbell rings and Tank leaves to go answer it. Another deep voice. It must be his brother. I grab the nearest dishtowel and hastily wipe my hands. Tank is so forceful. Such an enigma. I wonder what his brother is like.

I enter the living room. The guy on the couch looks like Tank so I know it must be his brother. "Hi, Finn. It's nice to meet you. I've heard a lot about you."

He accepts my hand and then doesn't let go so I'm forced to sit on the couch next to him. "My brother hasn't told me anything about you and I can guess why. Young. Beautiful. He's worried I'll steal you away."

"Yes, I am. So back off." Tank comes over and sits between us, forcing his brother to shift over on the couch.

"Boys, no fighting. You'll scare the poor girl off. I swear I raised them better than this Emma."

"Oh they're just joking around."

"I may be joking around but Tank is not," Finn whispers. I

glance at him and he smiles back. He's an attractive guy, much closer to the movie-star standard than Tank. But for some reason, I don't feel that wild, uncontrollable heat that I feel around his brother.

"Finn, help her set the table!" Claire scolds. He sighs and gives her a long suffering look but there's affection behind it.

"Sure thing." He walks to the cabinet against the wall.

As he walks, I notice that he has a slight limp. Then I remember that Tank put the cat's carrier near the cabinet. What if he falls over it or something?

"Watch out so you don't trip over—"

Finn's foot accidentally smacks into the carrier on the floor. Then he leans down to peer inside. "You have a cat? You don't have to keep her penned up." Before I can warn him, he unzips the case. "Come here, little kitty."

"You might not want to do that. Poochie's a little anti-social."

Finn looks back at me and winks. "Animals love me." He flips up the top flap of the carrier and suddenly there's a high-pitched screech. A second later, he jumps back, falling on his butt. *"What the ever-loving fuck is that?"*

"It's a cat. I adopted a cat," Tank mutters between clenched teeth.

"That is not a cat." Finn leans closer to get a better look. Poochie is now hiding behind the recliner in the corner. When Finn steps closer, she hops up to the top of the chair and hisses, her bony back arched. If she'd had hair to speak of, it would be standing completely on end.

"It's naked," Finn accuses before turning to look at Tank. "You have a naked cat?" Then he starts to laugh, his deep voice booming across the room. Poochie doesn't like the noise so she hisses again and then settles down on the back of the recliner with a haughty look on her face.

"Emma volunteers at the animal shelter." Tank looks vaguely embarrassed so I decide to help him out.

"Your brother was kind enough to help me out there yesterday. They're severely underfunded and there are so many animals that need help."

Claire puts her arm around me in a supportive squeeze. "That's so lovely that you volunteer to help out like that."

"Well, I want to be a veterinarian," I admit. "That's been my dream since I was a kid. I've always loved animals. But I wasn't allowed to have a pet because my mom was allergic to almost everything."

"Why don't you have one now?" Tank asks.

I take a deep breath. "Ivy isn't so fond of *critters* as she calls them. It's fine. Once I've saved up enough for my own place, I'm getting a dog. A big, sloppy, happy dog that will give me kisses when I come home."

Finn snickers. "Hell, you can just take Tank home with you if that's all you want."

"Finnigan!" Claire scolds but there's laughter in her voice as she says it.

I'm blushing but I'm laughing, too. "Anyway, the point is that

Tank helped me out yesterday and while he was there, Poochie took a bit of a liking to him."

"So you adopted it?" Finn looks back at the now snoozing cat in disbelief.

Tank shrugs. "The damn thing followed me around the whole time then looked at me like I was sending her to the gas chamber when I had to leave."

Finn looks between the two of us and then back to the cat before shaking his head in exaggerated wonder. "I'm just shocked. You've never been a cat person."

Tank looks over at me. "Apparently this is an exception."

My face heats under his scrutiny. His words from yesterday come back to me.

I just don't care that much as a general rule. You seem to be the exception.

I can't even begin to puzzle out what he means and what I want him to mean while under the watchful eye of his mother and brother. So I cough and step away.

"The bread should be about ready to come out of the oven. Excuse me."

* * * * *

I take the opportunity to check on the sauce again. The smell acts as a beacon and before long Claire, Finn and Tank are in the kitchen with me, gathering up plates and bowls and peering over my shoulder. It's a warm and wonderful feeling to have people to cook for again.

"It's ready."

Tank leans over my shoulder and I instinctively raise the spoon to his lips for a taste. His arms tighten around my waist and his head dips. We're so close, his chest to my back and his hips snugged up against my waist. My thoughts can't help but veer off in a different direction when he parts his lips.

Finn elbows him. "Get a room, you two. I'm starving."

The moment is broken and the murderous look on Tank's face makes up for the embarrassment of almost jumping him in his mother's kitchen. We all fill plates with pasta and bread hot from the oven. Once I'm seated, Claire holds up one of the wine bottles on the table.

"Red or white?"

"Red will go well with this meat sauce."

She pours a little in my glass and then some for herself. Tank brings out a beer for himself and one for Finn. He winks at me as he sits down.

There's no conversation for a while as everyone digs in. It's the most amazing sound for a cook when everyone is so absorbed with their food that they don't even stop to talk. I've outdone myself on the meat sauce and the pasta is perfectly al dente.

"This is delicious, Emma," Finn finally says around a huge mouthful of pasta. "You need to come around more often."

"Yes, she should." Claire sends a pointed look at Tank. "We'd be glad to see you anytime. That means bring her back, Tanner."

When she says his name, it reminds me that I wanted to ask her about it. "How did he get the nickname Tank?"

Tank looks over at me, surprised. "Why didn't you ask me that? I would have told you."

"Because I want to ask your mom. She'll give me the real story."

Finn snorts. "It's really not a story. He hit puberty and suddenly he hit like a tank. I had the bruises to prove it." We all laugh at his affected expression.

"You're hardly a small guy yourself. I'm sure you could handle it," I respond.

"True but not so much when he was fifteen and I was twelve. The story you really should ask Mom to tell you about is his skills onstage."

Tank drops his fork and glares across the table at his brother. "You really want me to tackle you right now, don't you?"

"The stage?" I look back and forth between them. "Was he in the school play or something?"

Claire takes a sip of her wine and glances over at Tank. "He used to perform with me sometimes when I was singing in a cabaret. I used to practice the songs all the time so I'm surprised Finn didn't know them, too. But Tank would sing with me. Once I realized he had talent, the theatre company cast him in a few small parts."

"That was a long time ago, Mom." Tank's cheeks have a slight flush to them. He's usually so nonchalant that I'm shocked he seems so bothered by this.

"Yes it was." Claire looks wistful. "I always wished I'd had the money to hire a singing coach for you, or something. He had a beautiful voice, even in high school. Some boys lose their voice after it changes but not Tank."

"Can we talk about something else now?" Tank looks mortified. "Let's talk about Finn and his extracurriculars in school. Oh wait, he didn't have any. Unless you count convincing girls to meet him under the bleachers."

Finn acknowledges the insult with a grin. "Hey, that was extra. And it was definitely curricular."

Claire puts down her fork. "Do I need to put you two in time out?"

"Okay, okay. So, how did you two meet anyway?" Finn takes a huge bite of his roll.

"Emma is a friend of a friend."

Finn looks confused. "What friend? None of our friends are classy enough to hang with her."

"I met Tank at the law office where I work. Actually, I know your father, too. He's been really nice to me. He gave me some advice about college. How to get loans and grants and stuff."

Silence descends upon the table immediately. Claire puts down her wineglass. "Their father? *Maxwell Marshall*? He's back in town?"

There's a sudden hostility in the air and I'm not sure how to answer. Tank and Finn seem to be having a silent conversation of some kind. Claire looks at me expectantly. There's a note in the air that I can't describe. This is more than just the usual post-divorce drama.

"Yes, ma'am. He's a client of the law office where I work."

She immediately looks at Tank. "This is why you've been so secretive lately? Oh lord, tell me that's not how you got the money."

Finn glances at me quickly before putting a hand on his mother's arm. "Mom, we don't want you to worry about any of that."

She doesn't answer and after a moment, gets up from the table. "Emma, I'm so sorry but I'm not terribly hungry anymore. I'm going to rest for a while."

"Of course." I watch as she disappears down the hallway leading to the back of the house. When I turn around, Finn's watching me with narrowed eyes.

"I didn't know it was a secret," I mutter.

"Don't jump down her throat, Finn. She's not the one in the wrong. We are. I should have told Mom last time I was here. She would have found out eventually."

"I know. But not right now. Not when she's already got so much to worry about."

Tank lifts his plate and his mother's from the table and disappears into the kitchen. After he's gone, Finn reaches out and touches my arm. "I'm sorry, Emma. It's really not your fault and I have no right to take my frustration out on you."

He gets up and leaves the table, too. I'm left alone with a plate of spaghetti and a half-empty bottle of wine. I pour myself a little more and take a swig before getting up to search for Tank. The back door is slightly open so I stick my head out into the cold night air. Tank is on the back step, leaning back on his arms and looking up at the night sky. At the sound of the door opening he looks over his shoulder.

"Sorry about the drama, Emma. I told you my family was like a reality show."

"You have nothing to be sorry for." I pull my sweater closer and then sit down on the top step next to him. I'd assumed he was looking at the stars but his eyes are closed.

"Can I ask you a question? And if it's too painful, you can tell me to mind my own business."

His eyes open and he angles his body so he's facing me. "You can ask me whatever you want. I've already told you, you're the exception to all my rules."

A thrill rushes through me at his words. It's impossible not to be affected when he's looking at me like this, like I'm the only thing he wants. The only thing he needs.

I look away and try to focus. "Why is this all such a big secret? I know your parents are divorced but was the breakup really that bad? He just seems so nice. I can't imagine Mr. Marshall doing anything to intentionally hurt anyone."

Tank leans back on his arms, his face turned up to the sky. "I'm sure he can seem nice when it's in his best interest. All the best con men are good actors. He fooled my mom into thinking he was a great guy until he ditched us when I was eight years old. Finn was five."

"He abandoned you?"

"Yeah. Never looked back either. I hadn't heard from him since until late last year when a letter showed up from a law firm in

California. I actually thought it was a scam at first."

"No contact in all that time? That's just ..."

"Pretty cold, right? But that's how he operates. Mom told us a few years ago that he actually came back once. It was a few years after he left. She didn't want us to know. Figured it was better for us not to be disappointed again if it didn't work out. That was a good call because it turns out he just needed money. He stayed in town long enough to seduce her and then he took her savings and cleared out again. That's what he does. He uses people."

All this time, I've been trying to put the pieces together. Why Mr. Marshall would be willing to pay so much just to establish contact with his son. Why Tank seemed so hostile toward him.

And why it all felt so wrong.

Now it makes sense. When I'd told Mr. Marshall that Tank flirted with me, I'd given him information that he'd seen as a possible weapon. He wasn't just asking me to carry a message to his son. He was using Tank's feelings for me to manipulate him.

And I'd played directly into his hands.

I turn to Tank and cup his face between my hands. He's startled but leans closer, turning into the warmth of my palm.

"If you don't want to see him, then you shouldn't have to. Do what your heart tells you to do and nothing less."

His eyes bore into mine like he's trying to read the truth of my words in my gaze. Then he leans closer. He glances up at me, giving me plenty of time to back away. To turn away.

But I don't.

His lips cover mine and soon my fingers get lost in his thick hair. His other arm lifts to hold me closer and the kiss deepens. When he kissed me before, it was all tangled up in heat and urgency. But this is completely different.

His fingers spread through my hair, holding me still as his tongue plumbs the depths of my mouth. All the while his thumb traces a soft path on my cheek. A soft noise escapes the back of my throat and the sound seems to spur him on. The way he touches me is so surprising. He treats me like I'm delicate, something he wants to protect but also like I'm the hottest thing he's ever seen.

Voices drift from the slightly open door behind us and then there's the clatter of dishes in the sink. The loud sounds remind me where we are. Claire or Finn could come out at any time and catch us. I pull back and take several deep gasping breaths. Tank is just as affected. His chest heaves and he closes his eyes, fighting for control.

I'd be a liar if I said it didn't give me immense satisfaction to watch this big, magnificent male creature fighting to control himself around me. But the longer I'm around Tank, the more I realize just how little possibility there is for us.

Even though he doesn't know it, I'm just one more person that Tank can't trust. One more person who wants something from him.

"I like you, Tank."

His eyes cloud and he pulls back slightly. "There's a 'but' in there somewhere. We're amazing together, Emma. I've never felt this kind of chemistry with anyone before. Have you?"

"No but that doesn't mean it's right. If it was any other time maybe I'd say we should just go with it and have a little fun. You're dealing with a lot and I'm still trying to get my education back on track. I think we need some time apart. To think. I don't have time for distractions and you have distraction written all over you."

The words seem to please him because he grins, that sexy, arrogant grin. "I'll give you some time. But I don't think it'll change anything."

"If we let it go any further, I'll only end up liking you more."

Suddenly his face changes. Becomes dark again. His mood swings are always so abrupt, they scare me a little. "I'm not sure I can stay away from you," he admits.

The confession rips at my conscience. He wouldn't feel that way if he knew why I was really here. Once he knows he'll hate me.

And that's what I'm really afraid of.

Chapter Ten

Tank

There's no right way to meet your father again. It's been twenty years since I've seen the man. But after my conversation with Emma a few days ago, I've made my decision. Spending time with my father will never be high on my priority list but getting medical care for my mother is. That's what my heart is saying loud and clear. Save Mom. And that's what I'm going to do.

Emma would be proud of my decision. I really wish she was here with me now. But she wanted time so I'll give it to her. Maybe she's right and it really is bad timing or maybe I just came on too strong. A family dinner may have been too much too soon. Plus all the drama at the dinner table would be enough to scare anyone off.

I knock on the door of my father's hotel room. A young woman answers the door. She leans back slightly at the sight of my scowling expression. I run a hand over my face and try to look neutral. I don't want to be here but that's not anyone else's problem.

"Tanner Marshall. Come in. Your father is expecting you." She leads me to a spacious living area. "Have a seat. He'll be out shortly."

The hotel is pretty swank. It's exactly the kind of place I'd expect him to be. "This is a nice hotel."

"Yes, it is. Mr. Marshall remodeled it last year." She smiles absently and then turns to leave the room.

"He owns the hotel?"

She gives me an odd look. "Yes, of course. He owns all of the StarCrest Hotels."

"Of course he does." Resentment festers just below the surface. Each one of these rooms goes for an astronomical rate. While my mom was clipping coupons and working two jobs, my father was buying hotels.

Briefly, I wonder if I'll even recognize him. My last memories of him were from the perspective of an eight-year-old boy. What boy doesn't think his father walks on water? But I'm a man now and I wonder what it'll be like to meet him again this way. Will he still seem familiar?

If I could have, I would have put this meeting off. Taken some time to prepare myself. But since I agreed to his terms, I have to meet with him in thirty days or less. I don't want to take any chances. If I keep to his agreed upon schedule then the money in my trust will continue to grow. So I'll visit with him until I have enough to pay for all of my mom's care. I may have to visit him to get the money but there's nothing in that paperwork that says I have to like it.

"Tanner. You're here."

I turn at the grizzled voice in the doorway. My face probably shows my surprise but it's too late to cover my reaction. When Patrick mentioned that my father was ill, it didn't really hit me that he would look sick. But this elderly man in a wheelchair is not what I was expecting. I don't bother correcting my name. He can call me whatever. I don't plan to be here enough for it to matter.

"Yes. I'm here."

"Would you like something to drink? They have lemonade. You always did like lemonade."

"I liked it when I was eight, Dad." The word slips out before I can stop it and it annoys me. I don't want to call him that. He hasn't earned the right to that title.

His face falls slightly but he recovers, wheeling himself over to the sideboard. He selects a decanter and pours himself a drink. "Of course. You'd probably be more likely to want a scotch right about now."

The fact that he's right only ratchets my irritation higher.

"Actually I don't want anything. I'm not here for a drink. You already know why I'm here. Mom needs surgery so I need the money. It's that simple."

"I don't have any right to ask but I'll ask anyway. Why does she need surgery?"

Keeping it a secret out of spite crosses my mind but who would that serve? He can't hurt her anymore at this point. Maybe if he realizes that she's sick and needs me, he'll let me out of these stupid scheduled visits.

"It's cancer. She has breast cancer."

He tosses the drink back but before he does, I see that his hand is shaking.

"My lawyer said she was sick. But I didn't realize it was cancer. I didn't realize." He wheels himself over to the window and looks out. In profile he looks almost sad. It's unsettling to see this display of emotion. I don't think of him as being sad or regretful.

In my mind, I am always eight years old and he is a spoiled, middle-aged man on a perpetual hunt for youth and excitement. The man before me now, this broken shell of a man, is someone that I don't know. His pain isn't something I want to see because it's so much easier to remember him as a bastard who walked out on his family than to see him as a man who regrets what he did.

"I apologize for forcing you into these meetings. But it was the only way that I could get you here."

"But why? Why was it so important for you to see each of us? And why the weekly visits?"

He doesn't meet my eyes. "I have my reasons."

His evasiveness pisses me off. Again, it's him pushing us around and structuring things to his perspective. He couldn't care less about how it affects me, Mom or Finn.

"I just wanted to see my children. I may have figured it out too late but you are my greatest accomplishments."

Despite the heartfelt speech, I can sense that there's a lot he isn't telling me. There's an ocean between us filled with half-truths and assumptions. It's like yelling across a great distance trying to be heard. And I find I'm just too damned tired to even try anymore.

"Well, you can see me but that's all. The papers said I had to show up. They didn't say I had to make small talk." I sit in one of the armchairs and glance at my watch.

Fifty-five minutes and counting …

* * * * *

After an uncomfortable hour staring at my shoes, I get up and leave. My father looks disappointed. I guess he thought that by forcing me to come here, that we'd eventually talk and make up. That an entire lifetime of him not being there could be erased with a pleasant afternoon.

I didn't take my bike today and I wish I had. A hard and dirty ride is exactly what I need to purge this restless rage from my blood. My thoughts turn to Emma. She's right, I know she is, that we need to keep our distance. But now I'm stuck in this endless limbo, wondering where she is and whether she's okay. That way lies madness so I decide to just drive.

I end up at Finn's place. His car is still in the same parking space. He must be leaving though since he's agreed to the weekly visits with dear old dad as well.

"Finn? Hello?"

He appears to my left, coming from the hallway leading to the bedrooms. "Hey. What's up?"

"Nothing. I just got back from seeing our father."

"No wonder you look homicidal."

I put my feet up on the coffee table. The television is on but the sound is muted. It's one of those news commentary shows where people are always yelling at each other and trying to sound more knowledgeable about world events than they actually are.

"I met our brothers. That was interesting." Finn sits on the couch next to me. He looks better. More alert. His eyes don't have the bleary quality they get when he's taking the pain pills.

"You did? When?"

"Right after you sent me the information. I drove over to their shop and we hung out for a minute. I would have gone with you that day if you'd told me."

I shake my head. "I wasn't sure if they'd be open to us. I was just feeling things out."

"They were cool. I have to admit it was weird to see that one that looks like you. Gabe."

I grunt in response. Finn narrows his eyes. "You're not listening to anything I'm saying. Why are you really here?"

"I have no idea."

"Where's Emma?"

"Again. No idea. Why would I know that? I took her on one date. One awful date and a do-over where I had to share her with a college boy and a roomful of feral cats."

Finn snorts. "You enjoyed it. And you even like that ugly ass cat you adopted to impress her. She's good for you."

"She's not my girlfriend Finn. She's not my anything."

"And therein lies the problem. You've been different lately. In a good way. I don't care what dumb ass excuse you're using not to be with her right now but just forget it. Call her up."

"She doesn't want me. Not really."

Finn gives me a disbelieving look. "Try telling that to someone who didn't see the way she watched you at dinner. I don't know how you two originally hooked up but she feels something for you. I'm not sure what, but it's something. And that's all you need."

He scrubs his hands back and forth over his face. "I can tell you from experience that looking back and wondering if you did all that you could sucks. You know what happened with Rissa. I still wish I'd fought for her. Don't do that to yourself. If things don't work out between you, let it be her fault, not because you didn't pursue it. At least then you'll have the comfort of hating her."

I'm stunned into silence. Finn doesn't talk about the past or what happened with his former fiancée. He blotted her out of his life so completely that it's almost like she never existed. This is the most I've ever heard him speak about it.

He raises bleak eyes to mine. "Call her." Then he gets up and walks back to his room. I let myself out.

I walk down the street leading away from Finn's place. Taking a drive would make more sense but I need the physical exertion. I want the burn of the cold air in my lungs when I breathe in. After I've walked for a little while, the neighborhood changes drastically. Graffiti pops up on random buildings and everything looks older. A man shuffles along pushing a shopping cart filled with old magazines and books. As I pass, he says "Change? Any change?"

I pat my pockets. "No, I honestly don't. Sorry."

He shuffles along with a disgruntled expression. I think about all the money sitting in my bank account now. I'm a freaking millionaire but I don't even have twenty-five cents in my pocket.

I laugh out loud. There's no one out here to see me laughing and talking to myself like a crazy person. Not that I should care. I have money. Isn't that supposed to make me happy? It's like I'm caught in a dream turned nightmare where on the surface I've been granted this amazing gift but it's just a facade. Because beneath it all, I don't have any of the things that really matter.

I'm not even sure how my phone ends up in my hand but suddenly I'm dialing Emma's number and holding on to the piece of metal like it's the only thing tethering me to the earth. Seeing her, hearing her voice is all I can think of. She's the one true and honest thing in my life. The only thing untainted by all the negative emotions I carry around like a suitcase.

"Hello? Tank, are you there?" Her voice echoes in my ear. I close my eyes and absorb the sound of her voice, the tones flowing over me and through me.

"I'm here."

She's quiet but I know she's still there. I can hear her breathing.

"Are you okay?"

I allow my head to hang loose on my neck. She's one of the only people content to just let me be. Not a lot of questions, just the important ones.

"Sorry. I know you said this isn't possible for you right now. And shit, I know I'm a bad bet any given day of the week anyway. I just needed to hear your voice."

"Tank," she breathes and that one syllable arouses me like she's talking dirty to me or something.

"I need you, Emma."

There's a rustle on the other end of the line. "Where are you? I'm coming to you."

I give her the address and then hang up to wait. The homeless man has moved on a little further down the street and it's just me and the concrete wall. I don't even want to think about my admission on the phone.

I need you.

There's usually a timeline of acceptable behavior in any relationship. You aren't supposed to need a woman that you've known less than a month. I should like her and want to see her again but need her?

I push off and decide to circle the block again. She won't be here for another few minutes to pick me up. I haven't been walking long when I notice the man behind me. When I speed up, he speeds up. I turn another corner just to see if he'll stick with me. After a minute, he does.

He's following me.

I turn to face him. I could easily evade him but I don't want to run. I want the fight. *I need it.*

He seems shocked that I'm not running but recovers quickly. He pulls out a knife, the blade glinting in the moonlight. "Give me your money."

I attack first, rushing him and taking him back against the side of the building. A grunt escapes his lips as he hits the bricks. I must have knocked the wind out of him because he doesn't resist at first but then he headbutts me. He's strong but not as big as I am.

He's also slow. My fist connects with his ribcage, his gut and then his jaw. That familiar chill settles over me and I unleash all my rage, my frustration and my pain into hurting him. With my fists, I can right a few wrongs even if everything else in my life is going to shit.

"Tank, stop! You're killing him. Please." Emma's voice filters through the rage and I come back down to see the man is completely unconscious. I stagger back and collapse on the sidewalk.

"Oh my god, you're bleeding." Her hands come away from my arm smeared with blood. Until then I hadn't even noticed the searing burn on my forearm. He must have sliced me before dropping the knife.

"What were you doing?" she whispers. When I look up, she's watching my face closely. "You weren't even trying to get away."

I can't answer that but she must see the truth in my eyes. I wasn't trying to get away, I was *engaging*. I was participating.

I was enjoying it.

"We have to get out of here. You need to go to the hospital." She helps me to my feet, looping my good arm around her neck.

"No hospital. Just drive me home."

"But Tank, your arm—"

"*Please*, Emma. I need you."

The words hang there between us again and they take on a whole new meaning now. Her hand around my waist tightens."Okay, let's go."

The mugger's knife is on the concrete next to him. I kick it away and then pull away from her so I can lean down and rummage through his jacket. There's a wad of cash tucked into the inner pocket. Probably all the money he's stolen from other victims tonight.

"Tank! What are you doing?"

"Donating to charity."

As I walk away, I stuff the bills in the homeless man's cup.

* * * * *

Emma's hands are shaking as she grips the steering wheel. The look on her face back there in the alley. It was a kind of déjà vu. The horror and fear. Some of it directed at me. She's seen the real me now. She's seen the rage I can't control.

"Will you stay with me tonight?"

She hesitates and then I'm sure the answer will be no. There are reasons, valid reasons that it's a bad idea for us to get attached. She's trying to get her education back on track and I've already got my hands full dealing with my family situation. If we could have picked a worse time to meet, I can't think of when it would be. But none of that matters when I'm on the edge and all I want is to see her face.

"Yes. I'll stay with you." She glances at me once and then turns her attention back to the road. Her expression tells me nothing. Maybe she's staying with me because she's worried about me. I don't know and don't care. I have her for tonight and that's all that matters.

One more night of peace.

She pulls up in front of my building and parks. For a moment, I don't move, just sit watching her. I take a deep breath. The terrifying panic that's been riding me since I left the hotel recedes a little.

"Have you ever done the wrong thing for the right reasons?"

She's watching me with those big gray eyes and it feels like she can see straight through me. I've held it together until now but with one look, she disarms me.

"I would do anything for my mom, even make nice with my father, when I know he's up to something. But what if it's not enough?" My blurted words convey my deepest fear.

My anger toward my father has fueled me over the years, carried me through all the hard times, the loneliness, the worry that my mother was working so hard to take care of us. Letting go of that, even for a good cause, threatens my whole foundation.

If I don't hate him, then who am I?

My hatred has defined me for so long that I'm lost without it. Now I'm taking his money and allowing him back into my life.

What if I've sold my soul to the devil and it still doesn't save her?

"Let's go inside. I really want to look at your arm. I can at least clean the cut."

Once we're inside, Emma pushes me to the table. It's odd to submit myself to her care. She's never been the forceful type but my injury seems to have triggered her mother hen instincts. I show her where the first aid kit is located then sit as still as a child while she fusses over me, swabbing the long slice on my arm with peroxide and then wrapping it with an Ace bandage.

I could have done the bandage myself in less time and with a better result but it's oddly comforting to have her leaning over me, so concerned. Her warm manner wraps around me and pervades the darkness that's been in me since this afternoon.

When I agreed to see my father, I couldn't have anticipated the negative emotions it would dredge up for me. It's been years and I thought it was behind me. But there's no doubt that seeing him tonight has unleashed something in me. Something I'm not sure how to put back.

"Come on. Let's go to bed."

I don't even have the heart to tease her or make a suggestive comment. She tugs on my other arm until I rise from the table. Then she pushes me down the hall and into the bedroom.

She leans down and pushes her shoes under the bed. Then she takes off her earrings and opens the bedside drawer to drop them in. All the color drains from her face. She stands and backs away until she hits the opposite wall. Her breathing quickens, shallow breaths that sound like gasping.

"Emma, what—"

"I can't. I just can't." Then she bursts into tears.

My mouth falls open. The nightstand still hangs open so I walk over and peer in. My Glock 19 sits squarely in the middle of the drawer.

Emma turns to face the wall, still taking those rapid breaths. If she keeps sucking in oxygen like that, she'll probably pass out. I approach her slowly. My last girlfriend wasn't fond of seeing all my hardware either but she never reacted like this.

I want to hold her but I'm not sure if she would appreciate that right now. So I just lean on the wall a few feet away. "Take a deep breath. Slowly. In and out."

She looks at me briefly. "I'm okay. I just wasn't expecting it."

"I know. Just breathe, buttercup."

Her breath whooshes out all at once, and then she takes a deep inhale. Her eyes stay on my face. We stand like that for a few minutes, breathing quietly. When the color comes back to her face, I move away.

"I am so sorry. I'll move it." I lead her to the bed and she sits, woodenly. I block her view of the nightstand with my body as I retrieve the gun. There's a gun locker in my closet where I keep my Heckler & Koch and a few of my semi-automatic rifles. I walk into the closet and put the Glock in the case. When I come out, I sit on the edge of the bed.

"Emma? When your parents were killed … you were there,

weren't you?"

Her fingers clench in the blanket and then her head bobs up and down. *Yes.*

Emotion wells inside me. She's here, helping me, even though watching violence of any kind has to be traumatizing for her. The scene she witnessed in the alley tonight suddenly takes on new meaning. She waded into that for me.

She's dealing with things that obviously scare the shit out of her, *for me*.

"You don't have to stay. I understand if you want to go home." Even I'm not selfish enough to make her sleep here if she's freaked out. Nothing is going to help me at this point but I can help her. I'll probably be up all night anyway but she needs to sleep. And she needs to feel safe enough to do that.

She turns sad eyes to me. "I'm staying, Tank. I told you I would. I'm not going to leave you."

I'm not touching that statement so I grab a T-shirt from my dresser and hand it to her. She pulls it over her head and then pushes her jeans down. After she folds them and puts them on the end of the bed, she pats the space next to her. "Come on. I'm tired."

I don't believe that I'll actually get any sleep. When my emotions run high like this, sometimes I'm up for days on end. But the sheets are crisp and cool and Emma curls up next to me, warm and soft. Her bottom is pressed up against me and I'd have to be dead not to react to that but instead of it being purely sexual, it feels like she's an extension of me. Like she's supposed to be there. For the first time all day, I let out a breath and relax.

Then slip quietly into dreaming.

Chapter Eleven

Emma

This time when I roll over, I'm prepared for it. Tank is awake and watching me again.

"What is it with you watching me sleep? It's creepy."

He grins and pulls me closer. His morning erection pokes me in the belly. "Is that creepy, too?"

I rub up against him. "That part I don't mind."

He buries his face in my neck and inhales. It should be the weirdest thing in the world, curled up in bed with a man who is smelling me, but instead I feel safe. Protected.

"I'm starting to see what all the fuss is about having a

girlfriend."

"Now I know you're making stuff up. There's no way you've never had a girlfriend."

"Well, yeah. Of course. But I went in the Army straight out of high school. Most of my relationships were casual. It's hard to keep a girl happy if you're never around."

I'm fascinated by this side of him. Based on his behavior and well, just looking at him, I'd assumed he'd have had a string of girlfriends. Although I doubt he's been alone. He may not have had a steady relationship but I seriously doubt he's been living like a monk all this time.

"What about after you got out? You didn't meet anyone then?"

He sits up, dragging the blankets with him. "I met someone but after only a few months, she called it off. Said I was too much to deal with. In hindsight I don't blame her. You saw me last night. That's a lot to deal with."

"Do you do that a lot? Get into fights?"

He stretches his arms overhead, the muscles in his arms and back flexing. Looking at him like this, he's just overwhelming. He's like some kind of ancient warrior.

God, he's magnificent.

"Come on. We need to get up. You need time to stop at home for fresh clothes otherwise you'll be late to work."

I can tell he doesn't want to talk about it but this is too important. I won't let him sidetrack me. So I keep silent and wait.

He glances at me once more and then rubs a hand over his face.

"When I was younger, I used to fight all the time at school. I was on the verge of being expelled when my mom got cancer the first time."

"I didn't realize she'd had it before. You were so young. That must have been really hard."

"It was harder for her. That was the wakeup call I needed because I got my shit together and stopped making her life so miserable. She's been in remission until last month. That's when I started fighting again."

"You've done that before?"

He shrugs but when he looks over his shoulder, I can see the toll the admission takes on him. "I can't help her but I can help someone else. I can make something right in this world. I can do something that matters."

There's so much I want to say but I'm afraid of bungling it. I want to tell him how much he helps his mother every day. How strong he is for his brother and what an amazing friend he is, even to people who are just friends of friends like Sasha. He has this negative view of himself but he has no idea how I see him. How much he means.

"You matter, Tank Marshall. Just you. Not the stuff you do, although that's pretty amazing. I bet if I ask your mom, your brother and your friends what kind of man you are, they'd see the same things I do. Someone with great integrity who goes out of his way to help others."

"They'd do the same for me," he replies.

"Because they're your friends." I roll over so I can look directly at him. "And they're smart. They wouldn't be friends with someone who wasn't worthy. You are so worthy."

He leans back and I pull him against me. His head rests in the crook of my arm. "I'm afraid, Emma. This thing with my mom … I've never been this scared of anything in my life."

"I know. But every time you go out there and put yourself at risk, there's a chance that you won't make it back. Is it worth that? Think of the people you'll be leaving behind."

His eyes cloud and he suddenly looks far away. "My mom. My brother."

"Me," I whisper. "What would I do without my Tank?"

His eyes cut to mine suddenly and fix on my face with a surprising intensity. "Am I yours, Emma?"

There's nothing I can do to hide my feelings. He has to know how twisted up I am over him. "Sometimes I feel like I don't know what's happening with us. But I know that when you need me, I want to help you. The idea of you fighting really scares me. I don't want anything to take you away from me."

He sits up and pushes my hair back. His thumb traces a gentle circle on my cheek. The way he looks at me, I'll never get used to it.

It's like I'm all he can see.

He drops his forehead against mine. "Nothing is going to take me away from you. I won't let that happen. Leaving you is the last thing I ever want to do."

* * * * *

The woman who opens the door at Max Marshall's hotel leads me to the sitting area. I place my bag at my feet and try not to fidget. This morning with Tank was the most intense thing I've ever experienced. He's such a strong man. He doesn't allow himself many moments of weakness. I'm honored and humbled that he trusts me enough to be himself with me.

Which is why I'm here. I've known for a while that I can't take money from Tank's father. Not just because of how I feel about him but because of how I feel about Claire. How I feel about Finn. In just a short time, his family has become my family. I care about them.

I won't profit from something that hurts them.

But Max was my friend first. Even though I'm shocked and horrified by the things he's done in the past, I still can't help but hope that he's changed. Telling him that I can't help him in person is the right thing to do.

I glance at my cell phone to see what time it is. I meant to come at lunchtime but things were so busy at work today that I had to wait until I got off. If I don't get back to his place soon, Tank will worry.

"Emma!" Max wheels himself into the room. "What brings you by on such a lovely day? You should be out enjoying the sunshine."

"Hi, Mr. Marshall. Sorry for just dropping by. I hope I didn't interrupt anything."

"Nothing important. I'm always happy to see you."

He seems so genuinely pleasant. I watch him, looking for signs of greed or dishonesty. There's nothing to indicate that he isn't exactly what he seems: an eccentric billionaire who's pleasantly surprised by my visit. But after spending time with Tank, I have to wonder. I've gotten to know him. I've gotten to know Claire. She isn't the dramatic or overindulgent type. She wouldn't make up a sob story for attention or to gain sympathy.

The pain I've witnessed in their family is real and there's simply no denying that Maxwell Marshall is the cause of it.

"The reason I'm here is to tell you that I can't help you. With Tank. I like him. A lot, actually. I won't manipulate him. He's had enough of that in his life."

He watches me with unwavering eyes. "He told you, didn't he? That I left them."

"Yes, sir. It was hard for them. And I understand why he doesn't want to open himself up to a relationship that could end up hurting him again."

He looks sad but not surprised. "I can't say I'm not disappointed but I understand. You're a good person. I can see why my son cares for you."

I think back to this morning. Waking up with Tank. Talking about everything. The thing is, it's all so intense because a lot has happened over a short period of time. But I'm worried that this kind of intensity can't last. It comes on fast and burns bright but it can burn out just as quickly.

"I think your son is an amazing person. But we haven't known each other that long. And I know he doesn't trust easily."

He makes a sound of disagreement. "He trusts you. He doesn't take just anyone home to meet his mother."

I figured that was true by the way Claire and Finn responded to me. They'd seemed happy to meet me but also surprised. Suddenly it occurs to me that I never told Mr. Marshall about meeting his ex-wife. My eyes narrow. There's only one way he could have possibly known that.

"You've been watching him, haven't you? Does he know that you've been spying on him?"

"I'm a billionaire, my dear. And I have enemies."

"How long have you been watching over him?"

"Years. But he doesn't need to know that."

Again, I have the sense of being forced into the middle of a conflict between them. If I don't say anything, it feels like I'm deliberately deceiving Tank. But what would telling him accomplish? It'll only make him angry and he's already so angry.

I don't want to make any promises that I can't keep so I lean down to grab my bag. "I need to get back."

"Thank you, Emma."

It shouldn't make me feel guilty but it does. Why is he thanking me? I'm essentially telling him that he's on his own now.

"For what? I didn't do anything."

He gives me a sad smile. "Yes, you did. Sometimes the choices we don't make are even more important than the ones we do."

Before I have a chance to question that strange statement, he wheels himself to the desk against the wall. "Will you read some documents for me before you go? My eyesight isn't what it once was."

This I can handle. Despite knowing that his desertion devastated his family, I can't help my soft spot for him. I want to believe that he's as nice as he's always seemed but it's not my place to decide if he's really sorry or if he's really changed his ways. He'll have to earn his family's forgiveness, little by little.

"Yes. Of course."

He withdraws a sheaf of paper from the top drawer. "These. Can you read the name on each account please?"

"The Marshall Title Fund I and the other account is the Pacific Falls Investments. The first request is to add Damien Marshall. The second request is to add …" I stop when I see the name on the second form.

"Jonathan Boyd."

He doesn't seem surprised. "That's what I thought. I never authorized the second request. I was looking for something else in the files and found this. It's difficult to know who you can trust as you get older. There's a point where everyone around you is only there for what they can get from you."

His hand is shaking as he accepts the papers back. My own hands don't feel quite so steady either. The implications of this are worrying. Jon is stealing from him. I wonder if Ivy knows?

"Does he know that you suspect him? I don't want to leave you here alone if he's coming back."

He taps a button on his wheelchair. Instantly, the door opens and two large men come in. Max nods at them. "My security team is here.

Don't worry about me at all."

But even as he says it, he doesn't look comforted at all.

* * * * *

The trip home seems to take forever. My mind is on my meeting with Max and the papers he showed me. From the very beginning, I've been operating without all the pieces of the puzzle. All of Jon's snide comments make sense now. He's a thief so of course he can't understand why I'd be hanging out with Mr. Marshall so much. To someone like Jon, there's always an angle. He was probably worried that I'd see something I shouldn't while I was there.

Which turns out to have been a valid fear on his part.

As I turn down my street, my heart speeds up. I scrutinize all the cars parked near our house. Ivy's car is sitting in the driveway but Jon's car is gone. I let out a sigh of relief. He isn't here. I skip up the steps and open the door with my key.

"Ivy? Where are you? We need to talk." A door closes down the hall and I turn toward the sound. She must be in her room.

"I just got back from seeing Mr. Marshall. There's something I need to tell you." I rush into my room and grab my favorite pair of sweatpants and a handful of clean underwear. Bringing a suitcase would probably scare the hell out of Tank so I briefly contemplate doing it just for the entertainment value. Most single guys break out in hives at the thought of a woman taking over their space. So I just grab several skirts and blouses so I won't have to keep coming back for work clothes. I roll them to minimize the wrinkling and then tuck them into my messenger bag. If Tank needs me to stay with him, I'll be prepared.

I loop the strap of my bag over my head and walk back out into the hall. Jon stands in the doorway to Ivy's room. He's obviously just been asleep because his hair is rumpled and his eyes look bleary.

"Where's Ivy?"

He shrugs. "She needed something from the store. What were you yelling about? Something about Mr. Marshall."

"Oh, is her car having trouble or something?" I ignore his question and focus on a spot about a foot over his shoulder.

His eyes narrow. "Were you hoping I wasn't here?"

"Of course not. I was just wondering." My heart racing, I turn back and walk into the kitchen. I'm glad I didn't walk into the house and announce the news. Does he know, I wonder? Or suspect?

"What were you doing at Mr. Marshall's?"

"Just visiting." I open the refrigerator and pull out a bottled water. As I take a sip, his eyes follow the movement. I have to concentrate to swallow the mouthful without spilling any. His gaze is so smarmy. I feel like I need a bath just being in his presence.

"You seem to do a lot of visiting lately. A lot of talking. What do you talk about?"

"Nothing. Just school and stuff."

He steps closer, absently folding the cuffs of his shirt back. His eyes, hard and flat, stay on mine as he speaks. "You think I don't know what's going on there when I'm gone? You'd better not be lying to me, Emma."

It's foolish to provoke him when I'm here alone with him. But his manner just drives me crazy. "What we talk about is none of your business. I'm going to my room. When Ivy gets home, please tell her I need to speak with her."

I move to walk past him and he grabs my arm.

"Take your hands off me."

He yanks me closer. "What did the old man promise you, huh?"

Suddenly standing up to him seems like not only a bad idea but the stupidest idea I've ever had. "Nothing! I don't know what you're talking about. He's just a nice old man and I visit him sometimes. He's lonely and needs someone to talk to."

"That's how it always starts. He's lonely and he finds some pretty young thing to cozy up to. Did he tell you that you'd be his next wife?"

"No, of course not. He's old enough to be my grandfather."

"That's never stopped any of the others." His eyes travel the length of my body. "And you're definitely his type." His breathing changes, getting rougher. He's enjoying this and the thought sickens me. It gives me the strength I need to shove him away. Surprise works in my favor because he has to let go of my arm to keep his balance. I race for the door, leaving it hanging open as I jump over the top two steps and down to the lawn.

I'm in my car pulling away by the time he appears in the doorway. I watch him in the rearview mirror as I pull off.

Chapter Twelve

Tank

When Emma returns, she goes straight to the bedroom. I follow but stop when I see her sitting on the bed. She's texting. When she looks up, tears shimmer on her cheeks. She hasn't noticed me yet and I'm not sure whether I should give her privacy or just run in and grab her up the way I really want to.

Every instinct tells me that I should be in there with her, but whenever I get too close, she always pulls back. The last time things got intense, she asked for time apart. So even though it's killing me, I step back and retreat down the hall. Poochie curls around my ankles and lets out a garbled purr. I pick her up and carry her into the living room.

"You really are a funny-looking thing aren't you?" She grumbles and purrs under my hands as I stroke her wrinkled back. It's strange that despite how chaotic things have been lately, I feel more at peace now than ever. It makes no sense since I'm sitting alone on my couch with a cat that looks like a wrinkled old man, but the difference is I've made the decisions I needed to. I'm doing things with a clear head and focusing on what's important now instead of just reacting out of fear. And I have Emma. No matter what happens going forward, I have Emma.

The rest I can figure out as it comes along.

A few minutes later, she emerges wearing one of my old Army shirts and a pair of fleece sweatpants. Her hair is up in a messy bun and she's scrubbed all the makeup from her face. She's gorgeous.

"Are you okay?" I don't want to pry but she's clearly upset. I'm not sure what it is about this girl but just the thought of anyone hurting her makes me crazy.

She sits down on the couch next to me and gives Poochie an absent scratch behind the ears. "I can't find Ivy. She's always been a little flighty but she's been ignoring my calls since the weekend. I just don't know what to do. And Jon was there when I went to pick up some stuff."

My jaw clenches. "Did he say something to you?"

Her bottom lip trembles. "I know this is probably a little forward considering we've only been on two dates but can I stay with you for a while longer?"

You can stay forever.

The thought crosses my mind but I figure that would freak her out so I grab her hand. "You can stay with me for as long as you want."

"I'll start looking for a place tomorrow." She laughs suddenly. "We seem to do everything out of order. Our dates end up … not really being dates. I tell you we need to take time apart and I end up driving you home as you bleed all over my car. Now I'm asking you to move in because my sister's boyfriend is a disgusting perv. Nothing about us makes any sense."

"I want you with me. I don't care if it's bad timing or out of order or doesn't make sense."

Her eyes lock on mine. "You don't?"

"No. I don't. Break the rules with me, Emma."

She leans into me and we sink back into the cushions of the couch. Then she looks up at me with an expression of mischief on her face. "I'll help you out around the house. This place needs a woman's touch anyway. And another cat. I'll help you find a friend for Poochie."

When I look at her in disbelief, she buries her face against my neck, giggling uncontrollably. And it's the sweetest sound in the world.

* * * * *

Over the next week, we settle into a rhythm. I've never lived with anyone before. I was expecting the usual irritants such as someone moving things from where I've left them and having someone in my space. What I couldn't have predicted is the incredible beauty of having someone there when I get home. Someone who smiles at me with pure, incandescent happiness just from seeing my face.

I'm falling for her. Even more shocking, I'm enjoying it.

"Did you get the mail?" Emma grabs me from behind as soon as I enter the apartment. She smells like something spicy so I know she's been cooking again.

I hold up the stack of letters. Emma has forwarded her mail to my address temporarily so that she doesn't have to return home to pick it up.

"How are things with your sister?" From what I can understand, they still aren't getting along.

"Well, she finally returned my calls but she hasn't explained where she disappeared to or why she didn't call me back." She glances at me and then flips through the stack of letters, pulling out her bills. "She accused me of hitting on Jon."

"What? Why would she say that?"

"I'm sure he told her that. He's so sick. And very good at this game. Because he told her that, now she thinks anything bad I say about him is because I'm 'jealous and want him for myself.' Those were her exact words by the way." She smiles but I can tell how much it hurts her.

"I'm sorry. Hopefully she'll realize how wrong she is soon."

"She actually said that it was for the best if I don't come home for a while. Not that I want to be there." She rips open one of the letters and suddenly she's completely still. Then she crumples up the letter and drops it in the trash.

"Everything okay?" I watch as she opens the refrigerator and stands there, staring aimlessly,

"Yeah, fine."

I wrap her in my arms from behind. "Talk to me buttercup. And none of that *fine* stuff. Everyone knows that's woman code for *something is wrong, please ask me*. This is the one area where we've never been backward. You've always been honest with me. I think that's one of the things I love the best about you."

She stiffens in my arms. "I'm not perfect, Tank. Not by a long shot." She sounds so sad when she says it.

I squeeze her tighter. "I disagree. You told me I was an arrogant flirt. You forced me to realize how much my father's desertion bothered me. You've never held back on me before. Talking to you is the best part of my day."

She looks over her shoulder and then leans forward and kisses me on the tip of my nose. "It's just school stuff. I shouldn't let it bother me so much."

"Is it about your classes next year?"

She rolls her eyes but her nonchalant attitude can't camouflage the sheen of tears clinging to her lashes. "There might not be any classes next year for me. I didn't get one of the grants I applied for. It's the biggest one I'm eligible for so I'm just really disappointed."

My laugh startles us both.

She turns to me with a disbelieving look. The refrigerator door closes with a slam. "Did you just laugh?"

"Emma, baby, I'm sorry. It's just that … well, we've never talked about this. But I'm going to guess you know I'm not exactly *poor* since you know my dad."

"Yeah, I guess."

"Why haven't you asked me? You know I'd love to help you reach your dream. And I've seen you with animals. You are going to be a wonderful, compassionate veterinarian. Poochie and I are lucky to have you." I grin.

She doesn't smile back. "You can't give me the money."

"Why not? This is something I want to do."

"Maybe this just isn't meant to be," she continues. "Maybe this is a sign that being a veterinarian isn't what I'm supposed to do with my life. Is it crazy to keep trying for something when the universe is telling you it won't happen?"

"Or maybe this is a sign that you should learn to ask for help. Asking for help doesn't make you weak. It's okay to let someone catch you. To let me catch you."

"Why? So I can drag you down with me? So we can both sink?"

"No. So I can pull you up." I'm truly stunned. The idea of her turning the money down never occurred to me. I think of all the girls I've dated in the past. The thought of any of them turning down a gift is laughable.

"Well, I don't want you to do it. This is my dream and I'll get there through my own hard work. Not because my boyfriend bought it for me." She pulls away from me, and takes in several gasping breaths. "Oh god, this is just … I can't breathe."

I crouch down and peer into her eyes. She's flushed and still taking breaths like she's been underwater for hours. This is how she looked when she saw my gun in the nightstand. But there's nothing here that could possibly have scared her like that. "What's happening, Emma? Tell me what's going on?"

Her eyes look strange, the pupils slightly dilated. She sits down right in the middle of the floor and puts her head between her knees. Her breaths are coming a little slower now. She threads her fingers together and holds them behind her neck.

I sit next to her and rub her back gently. Once her breathing sounds more normal, she looks over at me. "Panic attack. They always hit me out of nowhere."

I wipe a stray tear from her cheek. "Are you okay?" Watching her suffering and not being able to do anything is excruciating.

"I'm fine. I just need a minute."

We sit quietly together, right there in the middle of the kitchen floor. "Everything is going to be okay, you know? School, work, all of it. You'll figure it out. I know you will and I'll be there to help as much or as little as you'll let me. You've got this, Emma."

"No. I haven't got anything." She leans against my arm and closes her eyes. "There's so much I wanted to do and I'm failing at all of it. All my mom wanted was for me to be happy. All my dad wanted was to watch me graduate. They would have hated that I dropped out of school and gave up on my dreams. I'm failing them.

There's just so much and I can't bear it."

I pull her on my lap so she's facing me. She chuffs out a little laugh and rests her forehead against mine. I remember doing this to her when I was the one having trouble holding it together. She helped me pull through that and I'll help her get through this. Whatever she needs me to do.

"You're not alone, Em. I'm here. You're trying to do it all by yourself but that's too much for anyone. We all need someone strong enough to hold us up when things get too heavy. Someone to be our anchor."

"Ever since my parents died, I haven't had an anchor. I'm just adrift. And when I fall, there's no one there to catch me. It's terrifying. There's so much and I just can't handle it all. All the worrying. Sometimes I think hitting rock bottom might be a relief."

"Then give some of it to me. Let me bear it for you. I'm strong enough. *I will be your anchor.* And I will never let you down."

* * * * *

There have only been a few times in my life when I've truly felt lucky. When my mom beat cancer the first time, when I found out that Finn survived the IED blast that almost took his leg and when Eli gave me a job so I could feel useful again. Those were times when I finally felt like someone upstairs was looking out for our family. Or at least not kicking us when we were down anymore.

But as much as I love my family and my career, they don't take away the loneliness I've felt all my life.

I look down at Emma, her eyes soft and languid as she leans against me. Maybe I've found what I need. What I need but didn't even know to look for.

"Come on, buttercup."

She doesn't resist when I lift her and carry her down the hall. She's so slim, almost too slim in my arms. It makes her seem even more fragile. The most fierce, protective feeling flows through me. I want to put her to bed and watch over her while she sleeps. Protect her and keep her safe from all the things that scare her.

Then she turns her head and takes the lobe of my ear between her teeth and that feeling morphs, shifting into the desire to take her. To keep her safe by keeping her under me.

We're on a collision course for the bedroom and I'm not stopping until I have her under me again.

She clings to me with her legs wrapped around my waist and her arms around my neck. Soft, fluttery kisses dance along my neck and then her hands are in my hair. She seems to particularly like gripping the thick strands at the base of my neck. Her breasts press against my chest teasing me with the stiff tips of her nipples. I can't wait to have the tight points on my tongue.

I push open my bedroom door and we tumble on the bed, a tangle of arms and legs. She rolls over and climbs on top me, running her hands over my chest. I sit up briefly to tug her shirt off. Her plain white bra is revealed. It's not meant to be sexy, just white cotton with no lace or details. With her flyaway cloud of buttery hair and the carnal look on her face, she looks like a naughty angel.

I dip my head and trace the plump flesh spilling over the cups before unhooking the clasp. She moans and her head falls back as I peel it down her arms, exposing miles of creamy skin. I breath deep, nuzzling against her throat. Being with her like this, touching her, tasting her, it's just as good as the first time. If I'm honest with myself, I can admit that I can't imagine it ever getting old.

I tug at the waistband of her jeans and she allows me to work them down her hips. While I strip out of my own clothes, she steps out of the little pink panties she's wearing. This time when she straddles me, there's nothing between us but skin.

I bite her on the neck and she cries out, the sound echoing in my ears. I take a deep breath, trying to calm down but the smell of her arousal curls through me, driving me higher. Her scent is intoxicating, warm and rich like vanilla.

"You are so beautiful. You stagger me." I take one of her hands and pressed it between my legs. There's nothing as arousing as the wonder and erotic curiosity in her big gray eyes as my cock juts into her hand. She caresses it lightly, learning the contours of its length. Then she grips it firmly between her fingers and squeezes. I groan as my cock jumps in her hand.

"You did that to me." I pull her down to the bed and run my tongue over the smooth skin of her stomach. She smells like spice and sin and tastes even better. I look up over the alluring curves of her body and watch as she arches into my touch. Talk about a hell of a view. With her neck bowed and her long hair curling against the creamy sheets she's like a siren in my arms, all fire and flame. I want more than just to have her for a tumble. I want to possess her. I want everything she has to give.

I slide my hands under her hips delighting in the way the soft flesh fills my hands. I squeeze the full globes of her ass, rewarded when she moans and tries to inch away from me. I swat the side of her thigh lightly. The look of shock on her face makes me laugh despite how turned on I am. My innocent little angel will be thoroughly shocked in every way possible if she keeps hanging out with me.

The pang that hits me in the chest reminds me of just how badly I want that, too.

"Tank, what are you doing?"

I turn her over until she lays on her front, the tempting lines of her back and ass now easily accessible. I take my time nibbling down her fragrant skin, teasing my tongue over the indentation of her spine. She arches and moans into the touch, her back curving like a cat in heat. When she moves that way her ass pushes back until it fits snugly against my cock.

"I'm giving you what you want. What I know you need."

She rolls over and raises an eyebrow. The low light filtering in from the open curtains is just enough illumination to highlight the creamy tones of her skin, the perfection of her form.

"What I need huh?" She props herself up on one elbow, her perky little breasts moving with the action. Its' all I can do to keep from leaning over and taking one of her nipples in my mouth. "I don't recall asking you for anything."

I grab a condom from the nightstand. She watches with interest as I roll it down my length. She wiggles her ass slightly and I move behind her again. I nudge against her wet folds, rewarded when she half shrieks, half moans at the contact.

"You will before this night is over. You'll ask me for things you never imagined." I move my cock around, playing in her moist folds but avoiding her clit, never quite giving her the stimulation she needs. One finger presses deep, and I grit my teeth as her body clamps down on the digit.

She's so tight. So fucking tight. I stroke her in long, slow measures using her body's moisture to ease the way. Before long her hands twist in the sheets and her skin gleams, damp with perspiration.

But she still hasn't asked for it.

I slip my hands underneath and cup her breasts. They tighten until her nipples are like stiff little berries against my palms. I pull back again, my cock sliding inside her a fraction of an inch. She stills, the muscles in her arms straining as she tries to push back against me. But I'm not letting her off that easy. It's too good, too hot, this erotic game we're playing. And I want her begging for it. I hold her off, sliding in and out in shallow thrusts, refusing to give her the deep penetration we both need.

"Stop torturing me." Her eyes betray her pleasure even as she's cursing me. She moans and gyrates her hips. She looks so sexy arching into it, her face so open and trusting. I love watching her eyes drift closed as I inch deeper. She whimpers and her mouth falls open on a pant as she fights for control. She's close. Too close. I pull out completely.

She slams a fist down against the bed in frustration and rolls over to face me. "Damn it, Tank. I'm asking okay. Please give it to me. *I'm asking.*"

The words are barely out before I plunge inside, stretching her legs back until they almost hit her shoulders. She gasps and wraps her legs around me, holding me against her as tightly as her pussy grips my cock.

It's like dying, a little bit at a time, or the burn of a blade right before the final cut. I'm fucking her hard, trying to put her through the mattress but I'm also trying to merge with her. Trying to make sure she never leaves me.

"You're mine, Emma. Mine."

She must feel it too, how close I am to going crazy because she strokes the side of my face, her eyes holding mine even as she starts to cry out, her own orgasm ripping her apart.

"I'm yours. Yours," she agrees. Then her eyes clamp shut as she shudders beneath me, her body clamping down on my dick like a tight wet fist.

"Jesus." I try to slow down, determined to draw out her orgasm but the tight contractions of her body are impossible to ignore. The familiar burn of my own release threatens, the pressure and heat gathering low, tingling at the base of my spine. She reaches behind me and clamps her hands on my ass, pulling me against her harder, forcing me deeper.

"I'm yours," she insists, "And you are mine."

That breaks me. As I come, my orgasm shattering me into a thousand pieces, I bury myself into her again and again and again.

Chapter Thirteen

Emma

The driveway is empty the next day when we pull up to my house. Tank didn't even want to come back here but I need to pack some stuff. I also need to check the mail for bills and information from the financial aid office at school. Even though my mail is being forwarded, I don't want to chance missing something major.

I get out and Tank follows. His eyes sweep up and down the street, scanning for threats.

"He's lucky he's not here," Tank mutters. He grabs the stack of letters and flyers stuffed into the mailbox and hands it to me. I flip through the stack quickly, pulling out anything that's addressed to me, and then put them in my bag. I open the door with my key and then put Ivy's mail on the hall table.

"Ivy? Hello?" After what happened last week, I'm not taking any chances that Jon might be here, even if his car isn't out front.

When we pass by the kitchen, I shiver thinking of what happened. Where is Jon now? And more importantly, where is Ivy? I won't rest easy until I know she's safe. If he got rough with me, then I have no doubt he'd do the same thing to her. If he hasn't been doing it already.

In my room, I point Tank toward my closet. He pulls out my battered brown suitcase and I start throwing in clothes. I skip the heavy winter stuff since it'll be spring soon and grab all my favorite skirts, slacks and cardigans. The rest of my stuff can wait. I'll have to get it when I have more time.

Tank watches silently as I pull out handfuls of lingerie to add to the pile and then rush into the hall bathroom to grab my toiletry bag.

"Let's go. I need to get you out of here before one of them shows up because I won't be responsible for my actions." He hefts the suitcase and I follow him out to the car.

Sadness descends as we pull away from the house. I grew up here. My last memories of my parents are in this house. But maybe that's why I need to leave. Staying here where the best and worst moments of my life occurred doesn't seem to be helping me move on. I lean against the window and watch the streets go by in a blur of motion. Before long we arrive at Tank's apartment.

"Home sweet home," he says.

"Just for a little while." There's no way this can be a permanent thing. He thinks he wants me to stay right now but that's only because he's never lived with anyone before. Once the shine wears off, he'll want his space and his privacy back.

He takes my suitcase in the house and deposits it in his room. "Do you want to go out for dinner?" His voice carries from the bedroom to the front where I plop down on the couch.

"That's fine." I pick up the remote on the cushion next to me and turn on the TV. It's showing a sports station. I flip channels until I find a home decorating marathon.

The stack of mail falls out of the top of my bag, scattering across the floor. Most of the envelopes are bills but the last one I don't recognize. I open the envelope. At first, I'm sure that what I'm seeing is a mistake. I didn't actually think this many zeroes could fit on a check. But there's no mistake and I can't even blame it on sloppy handwriting. It's a computer generated check from First National Bank and Trust for one million dollars. I find myself tracing the six zeroes over and over. Then the name on the account.

Maxwell Dean Marshall

I dig frantically in my bag for my phone. I'm not even sure exactly what I'm planning to do but I know that I have to give this back. Mr. Marshall must not have thought I was serious when I told him I wouldn't help him. Or it's some kind of mistake. Maybe he authorized the check before I came last week and didn't stop it in time.

I search through my contacts to find the number for his hotel. A man answers. The voice is slightly familiar but I don't have time to try to puzzle it out.

"Hi, is Mr. Marshall available?"

"No, he's not. Can I take a message?"

"Tell him that Emma is coming over. I need to give him something." I hang up before he can try to talk me out of it. If I have to I'll just shove the envelope into his hands and walk away. He's probably one of Mr. Marshall's many assistants. I don't care who takes the check as long as it's out of my hands.

"Tank, I have to go out."

He appears at my elbow, looking concerned. "What do you need? I'll drive you."

"It's personal stuff. I'll be back in less than an hour." I lean up on tiptoe and press a kiss to his lips. He softens slightly.

"Call me if you need me."

I grab my coat from the back of the chair and shove my arms into it. The cold air hits me as I rush out the door since I didn't even bother to button my coat. My car emits a soft purr when I turn the key. I gave Tank a hard time about it but I'm truly grateful. Whatever his friend did to my car, it's been running better than ever.

As I drive, my mind isn't on anything but getting to the hotel. How can I take anything from his father when I know now why Tank didn't want to see him? Although that's not the only reason I can't do this. It feels wrong to attach currency to any part of what I've shared with Tank.

How do you attach a price tag to falling in love with someone?

By the time I arrive at the hotel, I'm almost sick thinking about the envelope in my bag. I hand the valet my car key and run for the doors.

"Wait, Miss. Your ticket!"

"I'll be right back." I don't stop, barreling through the elegant lobby toward the elevators. The businessman on board looks shocked when I stick my hand between the rapidly closing doors.

"Sorry," I mutter before hitting the button for the penthouse. He glances at me from the corner of his eye and I use the time to slow my breathing. He gets off on the eighth floor and I ride the rest of the way up to the penthouse alone.

The doors open with a ding and I walk down the plushly carpeted hallway to the double doors. They open before I even get there. It's Jon. I stop, mid-stride. *Stupid stupid stupid.* No wonder his voice sounded familiar. I've only spoken to Jon on the phone once or twice.

"Emma."

I turn around to run back the other way. He's on me before I even reach the elevators.

"Get in here." He drags me back toward the hotel room. His hand clamps over my mouth so tightly that I can't even bite him. Once we're in the suite, he kicks the door closed behind us. The main living area is empty.

"If you hadn't hung up on me, I could have told you that Mr. Marshall is in a meeting across town. You're too late." He's talking to me in the calmest voice, as if he's not holding me in a stranglehold.

"You know it's interesting how after visiting with you, suddenly the old man decides to do independent audits on all his accounts. Am I supposed to believe you two are just besties now, huh? What happened Emma? Were you worried there wouldn't be any money left before you could get your hooks into him?"

I scream against the back of his hand. He squeezes my jaw so hard my teeth grind together.

"Shut up, bitch. I know what's going on now. I saw the check, Emma. You can drop the innocent act."

I stop struggling momentarily. He knows about the money? I didn't think Mr. Marshall would have told anyone about it. Isn't it illegal to do stuff like this? Then I realize he's a very rich man and probably used to giving people large sums of money all the time.

I struggle against him and try to elbow him. He snickers. "I just figured you were cozying up to the old bastard so he'd pay your rent for a while. Or give you some money for tuition. But a million dollars? You're smarter than I gave you credit for."

His arms tighten around me. I can feel his breath, hot on the side of my face. A ripple of disgust rolls through me.

His hand has finally loosened slightly so I wrench my head to the side. "I don't want it! If you're the one who sent it than you can take it back."

"Let me guess, you want more? You probably figured a million isn't enough for a rich old codger like Mr. Marshall. Well, I protect him from greedy bitches like you every day."

In his mania, his grip has loosened enough that I can lift my leg a bit. I raise my foot and stomp down on his toe. He stumbles and I run to the other side of the room, so the couch is between us.

"Protect him? You're stealing from him." I look back and forth between where he's standing and the door. My heart is pounding so hard that I can barely breathe.

"You'd better not be thinking of going to the media with this."

"That's not why I'm here. Just tell Mr. Marshall that I don't want any parts of this. I'm tearing the check up."

He leaps forward over the couch and manages to snag the edge of my coat. I fall backward into the coffee table.

"Get away from me!" I roll away and try to pull out of his grasp. Then he's on me, holding me down. I can feel the imprint of his arousal. He laughs and grinds it against me. As we struggle, something falls and crashes to the ground. Pieces of crockery land next to me.

Voices sound outside the door in the hallway. Jon looks up and I grab one of the sharp pieces on the floor and swipe out blindly.

"Aah!" He falls to the side clutching his face.

I jump up and race for the door, pushing past the redheaded woman who has just entered.

* * * * *

The bellman in the hallway jumps out of the way as I burst through the doors and run for the elevator that just opened. I know what I must look like with a fresh bruise on my cheek and my blouse hanging open. I bang the buttons rapidly until the doors close.

"Get back here, you crazy bitch. She attacked me. Stop her!"

I can hear Jon's voice getting smaller and smaller as the elevator descends.

When the elevator car finally reaches the lobby, I run past the small crowd waiting to get on. There are a few shouts and gasps as I shoulder my way through. Outside, I step directly into a cab at the curb.

"Go! Quickly."

The cabbie pulls out into traffic. I turn back to see Jon racing out of the hotel. He stands on the curb looking in both directions.

Back at Tank's place, I immediately go to the bathroom and strip. I just want a shower. I step into the stall before the water is fully warmed up. Cold water splashes over me and I duck my head, allowing the stream to saturate my hair. After a few minutes the water warms up and I rub my arms briskly, trying to lose the chill.

"Emma? I heard you come in."

It takes me a minute to find my voice. "I'm here."

There's the rustle of fabric and then the curtain moves to the side and Tank steps in behind me. As soon as he touches me, I turn and plaster myself to him. He pulls back slightly and holds my shoulders. Suddenly, his entire body goes rigid.

"What the hell happened to your face?"

A sob escapes my lips and Tank brushes my wet hair back. He tenderly lifts one of my wrists. Black and blue bruises are already showing up.

"Emma? Did Jon do this to you?"

I nod silently then bury my face in his neck. He holds me and then suddenly squeezes me tightly. "I am going to hurt him. He will pay. I promise you that."

"I don't want you fighting."

"There's no stopping this, Em. He hurt you. I can't stand it, can't live with knowing that he did this to you. Why did you go back there without me?"

My muddled mind finally comprehends that he thinks Jon was at my house.

"You don't have to talk about this. Come on. You're shivering." He cuts the water off and extends his hand to help me out of the shower. He wraps a thick towel around me and gently blots all the water off. Then he scrubs himself quickly with the same towel and wipes it over his head roughly.

"You need to rest." He picks me up and carries me to his bed.

I curl around him. I push my face right up against his broad chest, reveling in the scent and warmth that is uniquely Tank. Just a few weeks ago, I barely knew him and now he feels like my lifeline. A soft melody reaches my ears and then words. He's singing to me.

His voice is warm and rich. It wraps around me as tightly as the blanket. It's not until the tears flood my eyes and drench the pillow that I realize I'm crying. I don't deserve this beautiful man. Because he has opened his soul to me and I'm lying to him.

It hurts imagining what it'll be like once he knows. He'll hate me. I never knew I could be devastated by something that hasn't even happened yet. But that's what this feels like. Devastation.

Like I'm already in ruins.

Chapter Fourteen

Tank

As I walk through the corridors of the hospital trying to find the signs leading to the billing office, I mentally calculate how long this trip will take. Leaving Emma after what happened last night was the last thing I wanted to do, but the first installment payment from my father hit my account this morning. Finn and I can finally clear the latest round of my mom's medical bills.

"She's fine, you know. She's safe at my penthouse. You need a keycard to reach that floor."

"Yeah I know." What he doesn't get is that I can't take chances with Emma. Just the thought of anything happening to her … is unimaginable.

"Here it is. Billing." Finn points at the sign on the door to our left.

We enter the small waiting room. The young woman behind the desk perks up and directs her smile at Finn.

"Can I help you?"

"Yes, we're here to arrange payment on our mother's account." Finn pulls the last hospital bill printout from his pocket and slides it across the desk to her.

She glances at me briefly and then turns to her computer. A few key taps later, she frowns. "The balance on this account has already been paid."

"What?" I lean over the desk and try to see the screen of her computer. "It hasn't been that long since we got the last bill. Who paid it?"

"Sir, I really can't give out patient information. Someone in your family must have gotten their wires crossed. But you'll have to deal with it directly or your Mom has to authorize us to speak with you about her account."

Finn leans over the counter, all smile and charm. "It's okay, sweetheart. It's probably just our father. It's Maxwell Marshall, right? That's our dad. Usually we handle all these details but he must have gone ahead and taken care of it for us."

She visibly relaxes. I can practically see her melting in front of us. Finn tends to have that effect on women. "Oh good. I'm glad."

"Thank you for your help ..." His eyes drop to the nametag

pinned above her left breast. "Ms. Weston. We really appreciate it."

As we walk away, I ask, “How did you know it was him?”

Finn glances behind him. The nurse is still watching us. He waves and she smiles back at him. “Who else would it be? Not that many people know she’s sick and even fewer have that kind of cash. He’s probably just feeling guilty. Whatever. I don’t care why he did it. I’m just glad he did.”

“Yeah. Me too. I’m just surprised.”

“All right. I’m out of here. I have an appointment in a half hour.” He seems nervous and something about that dings my internal radar.

“What’s up with you today? You seem anxious about something. What’s this meeting for?”

“It’s nothing. Just meeting up with an old friend. I’ll see you later, Tank.”

* * * * *

The woman who answers the door of my father’s hotel room is about my age with wild red hair. I’ve never seen her before. I guess I should get used to this. My father is a rich man and he seems to have any number of people working for him.

“Uh, hi. I’m here to see my father. Is he here?” I probably should have called ahead but I was going on instinct.

“You must be Tank. I’m Charlene, your father’s personal assistant. He’s handling something right now but I’m sure he’ll want to see you. Follow me.”

His personal assistant. I wonder what the other lady was. His second assistant? Assistant to his personal assistant? Is this what I'll be like in twenty years? It's a strange thing to think of the future now. There was a time I wondered if I'd live to see thirty at all. Longevity isn't assumed when you spend your time watching the world through a scope.

But I have an entirely different future to look forward to now. Since my mom's astronomical hospital bill was cleared, I can use my money to set up the other treatments she needs. We can afford for her to complete chemotherapy and even try some of the therapies offered overseas. Things that aren't approved yet in the U.S. but have been saving lives in other countries.

I'm not used to feeling gratitude but that's what this is. He's given me back my hope for a little while. The least I can do is say thank you in person.

It makes me feel guilty that I assumed he was so cold. He's asked for very little actually. He just wanted to see me.

As we pass through the outer doors into the main area of the hotel suite, there's a sudden, loud voice. The door to one of the bedrooms opens.

"Don't think this is the last you've heard from me, old man. I know *everything*." Mr. Boyd exits followed by two of the big, burly guys I remember from last time.

As they pass, Boyd points a finger at me. "He manipulates everyone around him. Don't for one minute think you're any different."

One of the guys grabs him by the arm. "Come on. You've said your piece."

"He hired that girl to draw you in and it worked. But he'll get rid of you just as quickly as he did me when he's done with you."

I reach out and grab his arm. He's so startled that he halts his tirade. I hold up a hand to the two security guys. "Wait a minute. Let him speak."

His skin has turned a sickly shade of green under his spray tan but he must sense this will be his only chance. "You should know the truth about him. He uses his money to control everyone around him, including his children. He probably figured one million was a cheap price to pay to get you right where he wants you. You're a fool if you believe otherwise."

Everything inside me shrivels up into a little hard ball. "You said he hired "that girl." What girl?"

"Emma Shaw." He sneers her name and I immediately want to wipe the syllables from his mouth. It's wrong for him to even speak her name. Not to mention the unholy look in his eyes.

"What does Emma have to do with anything?"

He laughs and my hands clench into fists.

"You actually thought she cared about you? Girls like that start coming out of the woodwork when you have money. I'm doing you a favor. At least you didn't marry the bitch. That's what he would have done."

He's goading me and I know it. My mother is one of the women he's referring to. It would be foolish to respond to the obvious taunt.

He wants me to hit him so he'll have something to use against me. I need to walk away. Be the bigger man.

Then I think about it again and decide, *Fuck it.*

I punch him right above the nose. He buckles and drops to the ground like a stone. "I wouldn't be here if he hadn't."

The two security guys are grinning at me now. "I'm done with him. You can take him … wherever you were taking him."

I honestly don't care at this point.

The door to the bedroom they just exited hangs open. My father is sitting next to the window. He turns his head as I enter the room.

"Tanner? What are you doing here?"

"I was coming to thank you for paying mom's hospital bill. I had this whole speech worked out in my head about how I'd misjudged you and you really were just looking to start over with us. Then I find out that you hired Emma to what, to seduce me?"

"It wasn't like that. Emma is a nice girl. It was an opportunity for her to earn some money for her education."

"Normal relationships don't work like this. You can't just pay people to be your friend or to do what you want. That's not how it works."

"I didn't mean to cause trouble between you two. That's not what was supposed to happen."

His words only fuel my anger. Things always happen the way he wants them to and no one ever says no. Money has greased the wheels of his life for so long that he doesn't know how to operate without using it. He doesn't know how to have a normal relationship based on give and take.

"You want to know why you don't have family around to take care of you while you're sick? Because of shit like this. You manipulate people and use them to get what you want. You're like a cancer. A sickness that spreads and devours everything around you. You wonder why you're all alone? *This is why*."

His mouth opens and then closes again but no sound comes out. His skin pales even further until he looks almost gray. My anger recedes as I realize that he isn't responding to anything I've said. Not the anger or the accusations.

He looks stricken. For a moment, I feel guilty for how I'm lighting into him. He looks old and frail. His hand is shaking when he puts it to his forehead.

"Well? *Say something.*"

The hand resting on the side arm of his wheelchair shakes before falling to the side. His entire body slumps over, his head falling forward wildly.

"Dad? Help! *Somebody*."

The doors to the suite burst open. The redhead who answered the door looks between me and my father in shock.

"Call 911."

She recovers then dashes to the phone on the table. While she's dialing, I press my fingers to the side of my father's neck. I can't feel anything and I'm not sure if it's due to the angle of his body or the adrenaline racing through my own veins.

"Come on. Come on."

* * * * *

At the hospital, the doctor disappears behind the swinging door and leaves me standing in the waiting room feeling like someone just clawed an open wound in my chest.

He's alive. Barely.

"Is there someone I can call for you?" The nurse behind the desk is watching me with the kind of patient, gentle expression I imagine they must teach at nursing schools. She's an older woman, with dark brown hair pulled up into an elegant knot at the back of her head. She looks like the kind of lady who has a husband and three well-behaved kids. I briefly consider asking her if she'd adopt me.

I wouldn't even know what to do in a normal family.

"No. I'm going to call my brother." I pull out my cell phone and retreat to one of the uncomfortable waiting room chairs. I dial Finn's number and the voicemail picks up.

"Finn. I'm at the hospital. Norfolk General. Our father has had a stroke. Or a heart attack. I don't even know exactly. I just … need you to come. Just in case."

I hang up and scrub my hands through my hair as I settle back to wait. The time passes slowly. I've never liked hospitals and this waiting is just brutal. I look at the clock on the wall for the millionth time. The doctor still hasn't come back out to tell me what's going on. I've been waiting for a half an hour. I glance at the nurse behind the desk. She looks at me and then her gaze skitters away.

I pull out my phone again. Shouldn't there be someone else I should call? Does my father even have friends? There are probably a million things I should be doing right now but I have no idea what they are. Things a good son would do. But then I'm not a good son, am I?

I was yelling at him. *Christ.*

The door from the outer corridor opens and Finn walks in. A second later, Gabe and Zack follow.

A sense of relief fills me to overflowing. I sit down suddenly, sagging against the chair.

"I came as soon as I got your message." Finn takes the chair next to me. Gabe and Zack take the ones across the aisle.

"How is he doing?" Gabe asks.

"I don't know. They won't tell me anything." My voice cracks slightly.

Finn's hand lands on my shoulder. "He's going to be okay. He's too cranky to die. Isn't it only the good who die young?"

I know he's trying to make me feel better but his words just work on the guilt I'm already feeling. "I was yelling at him. I told him he was a bastard who would die alone."

"It's not your fault."

I look up at Zack's voice. Gabe and Finn look over at him, too. He speaks so rarely that it's always something of a shock.

Gabe grins at us. "Yeah, he comes out to play sometimes."

"Shut up, Gabe," Zack responds, but there's a wealth of history behind it. It reminds me of how I fight with Finn. "All I'm saying is, it's not your fault. Any one of us could have been there when it happened. Hell, I yelled at him when I saw him, too." He runs his hands over his shaved head. The intricate designs tattooed on his scalp stand out in stark relief against his pale skin.

I glance over to see Finn watching me. "You guys were getting along better. There's got to be more to this story. What happened?"

Strangely enough, I have somehow pushed the conversation about Emma to the back of my mind. "It was about Emma. He hired her."

I stand up. I just can't sit in these stupid beige chairs any longer pretending like everything in my life isn't completely screwed up. The one person I thought of as normal, perfect and untouched has been a part of this screwed up business from the beginning.

"He hired her?"

"According to Mr. Boyd. But Dad confirmed it." I give a bitter laugh. "He paid her to convince me to agree to his terms."

Finn blows out a breath. "Damn. That's pretty cold."

"He said that he wasn't trying to cause trouble but I can't trust anything that comes out of his mouth. I'm not sure what's really going on but we should probably all be on guard. He has his motives for bringing us back into his life."

"Tank! Finn! I got up here as soon as I could."

For a brief moment, my heart lifts at the sound of her voice. I guess it hasn't gotten the memo yet that she's not really ours. She's not really mine.

Finn turns apologetic eyes to me. "She was in the shower when I got your call. I told her to meet us here." He glances over to Gabe and Zack. "We'll go get some coffee."

Emma looks between us uncertainly. She can surely feel the difference in the way Finn is treating her. He doesn't even look at her on the way out.

"How is he?"

"Are you asking for my sake or your sake?"

She looks puzzled. "Both. I want him to be okay, too."

"So he can pay your salary?"

She freezes and her eyes lock on mine. "No. It has nothing to do with that."

I am so fucking wrecked over this girl. It kills me that she still has secrets. But I'd only known her a month before we started hanging out. The fact that she occupies most of my waking thoughts doesn't make me an expert either.

"I know about the money. Jonathan Boyd told me all about it. That's what caused the argument that gave my father a heart attack. We were fighting over you."

She flinches as if each word pierces her through and through. Even though I know she's a liar, I want to pull her close and shield her from pain. Because this hurts. This really fucking hurts.

"I told him that I didn't want the money. That I just wanted you. You've had so much loss in your life. I didn't want that again for you."

"Loss? Yeah I've known loss but that doesn't mean I didn't believe what we had could last. I know that not everyone is like my dad. My mom stuck around and she took the best care of us that she could. My daddy issues don't blind me to reality. Plenty of people find a person to give a damn about that manages to stick around. This isn't about my family. It's about me and you."

She pales. "I know. It's about how I screwed up. That's why I didn't want us to get involved. But I just couldn't stay away from you. Every time I wanted to move away, you just pulled me back in."

"You know, I told myself not to fall for you because it was too soon and the risk was too high. These kinds of whirlwind things never last. But somehow, with you, I thought it was a risk worth taking. I thought we would be the exception."

In the sudden silence, I glance around. The other people in the waiting room are watching us with wide eyes and open mouths.

I grab her by the arm and pull her into the stairwell. "Tell me the truth. All of it."

"When your dad offered me all this money just to ask you to meet with him, I thought it was the answer to my prayers. We're friends, I didn't lie about that. I thought he was just a sad old man who wanted to reconnect with his family."

"That's why you suddenly wanted to go out. For the money."

She looks up at me, her eyes swimming with tears. Her face is a mask of guilt and confusion. But I can't think about whether she's sorry yet when I'm still not clear about what she's done. If we're going to rip the wound open, I'd rather do it all at once.

"It was more than enough money to pay for my undergraduate degree and my tuition for veterinary school. It was a chance to start over. All for nothing, really. Just talking to some guy and asking him a question. I wasn't prepared for things to get so complicated. I wasn't prepared for … you."

Her answer stuns me into silence. But I can't deal with that. Not here. Not now.

"Yesterday, I tried to give the check back but Jon ..." Her face crumples.

"He was there?" Then I close my eyes. I have truly been blind this whole time. "Your sister's boyfriend Jon is *Jonathan Boyd*, my father's lawyer. Of course."

She nods, tears slipping down her cheeks. "Yes. He thought I was trying to get more money. I was just trying to give it back."

"My father's security guys told me that he has an open warrant in another state. I'm sure they were the ones who told the authorities where he was. He's in jail now but if I had known … *fuck*. I had that guy right in front of me. I should have done more than punch him. I'm going to kill him."

She clutches at my forearms. "I don't want you to kill anyone. I didn't want any of this."

The door behind us opens, the light from the waiting room spilling into the dark stairwell. The brunette nurse looks between us uncertainly. "Mr. Marshall. Your father has just woken up. He's asking for you."

I turn back to Emma. "I have to go. Will you … where will you be?"

"This is a family thing. I shouldn't be here. Go and be with your brothers. And here." She pushes an envelope into my hands. "I don't need this. I never did."

I stuff it in my pocket without opening it.

"Tank?" Emma is watching me, her eyes sad. "Even though he was wrong to do what he did, I think this is what he really wanted." She points at me and then at Finn, Gabe and Zack standing just inside the doorway.

"I think he just wanted to bring you all together, before it was too late."

Chapter Fifteen

Emma

I leave the hospital and it feels like I'm escaping a war zone. The woman who interrupted us gives me a sympathetic look as I pass the nurse's station. I probably look like hell. I press the backs of my hands to my eyes.

My eyes already feel swollen.

Outside on the curb, I pull out my phone and call Sasha. When it goes to voicemail, I hang up and reluctantly call Ivy. She hasn't been there for me in the way that family should be lately but she's still my sister.

And she's the only family I have left.

It rings several times. When the voicemail picks up, my heart sinks. Are we back to that already? She's not going to answer my calls. I don't want to go back home. Even though Jon is in jail, I don't feel like I belong there anymore.

I look behind me at the double doors leading into the hospital lobby. The only place I want to be is back there in that waiting room with Tank. He looked so devastated. So broken.

My phone rings in my hand and Ivy's number pops up. I answer it immediately. "Ivy?"

"Emma? What is going on? Jon just called me and asked me to bail him out of jail."

"You didn't do it, did you?" Sudden panic closes my throat at the thought that Jon might be out roaming the streets freely.

"No. We're not together anymore. So much has happened, Em."

"Yeah for me, too. It's a long story. Can you come get me? I'm at the hospital."

She agrees and I sit on one of the metal benches out front to wait. Fifteen minutes later, Ivy pulls up in front of the Emergency entrance. I run over to the passenger side and get in the car.

When she sees my face, she gasps. "Oh my god, Emma! What happened to you?"

"Jon happened to me. He was at Mr. Marshall's suite when I went there yesterday. It's a long story but he's been embezzling from Mr. Marshall and he thought I was going to tell the media."

She lays a hand over the bruises on my wrists. Then her lower lip trembles. "What have I done?"

Whatever I was expecting when I called her, it wasn't this. "Ivy, it wasn't your fault."

She clenches her hand into a fist. "I brought him into our lives. Our house. You tried to warn me so many times and I didn't want to hear it. I didn't see how right you were until he hit me. I had never seen him like that. I'm so sorry I accused you of being jealous when you called. I already knew what kind of person he was but I was ashamed to admit that I'd been so wrong about him. I've been staying with a girlfriend for a while since he kept coming by the house. That's why I told you it was better if you stayed away. I didn't want you there dealing with him either."

"We've both made mistakes. I did something. I didn't tell you the whole story that day when you picked me up from Tank's apartment."

"I know I haven't been a good sister but you can tell me. Tell me now." She puts the car in gear and pulls off. "I'm not going anywhere for a while."

That actually brings a smile to my face. It's something the old Ivy would have said. The real Ivy. The sister I haven't seen in almost a year.

"Mr. Marshall was my friend. But he was also using me to get to Tank. He offered me money to act as a liaison between them. All he wanted was for me to figure out why Tank was so angry and convince him to give his dad another chance."

"How much are we talking here?"

I roll my eyes. "Some things never change. That's not relevant."

"It is. Because if it's as much as I'm thinking it is, then a lot of things are starting to make sense. Jon was obsessed with you. I was … I was jealous," she admits. "I can't believe I listened to the things he said about you. That you were coming on to him. That you wanted him for yourself. I let him poison me against you. I was so stupid."

"I've been plenty of stupid lately myself." I think back to that moment when Mr. Marshall first offered me an "opportunity." If I could have ever guessed the wild twists and turns my life would take as a result of that one choice.

"I shouldn't have done it. I should have said no right then and there."

That's when I lose it. I'm not much of a crier. I usually bear things in silence or in the privacy of my room. But when I think about Tank, how I've hurt him, I just lose it. Ivy watches in shock and then pats my back awkwardly.

"I've never seen you like this."

"I hurt him so much. It kills me that he's hurting. Even more that I've caused it. I should have known that there's no such thing as easy money. Everything comes with a price and apparently the price of my stupidity is hurting people that I've come to care about."

I can still remember the expression on Finn's face. He was uncomfortable and embarrassed. But he was also hurt. He'd looked truly hurt. I don't even want to imagine how Claire will feel when she finds out. The choices I've made have done a lot more than just torpedo my relationship with Tank. They've destroyed my newfound family.

"You must really love this guy." Ivy glances at me with something akin to fascination. Once we stop at a red light, she digs in her purse and pulls out a small pack of tissues.

I yank out a few and press them against my eyes. "Not that it matters now. I've killed any chance we might have had."

She shakes her head. "No more talk about men. I'm going to put you in some warm pajamas and then I can finally start being a big sister again."

"Which means, what?"

"Ice cream, of course. Lots and lots of ice cream."

* * * * *

Ivy digs out a huge spoonful of Rocky Road. "This is the best breakup cure on the planet. Why can't I just marry Ben and you can take Jerry? We'll be happy for the rest of our lives."

Sasha holds up her spoon in agreement. "And they would never betray you."

Even I have to smile at that one. When Sasha called me back, somehow the entire sordid story came spilling out. I was so choked up that Ivy had to take the phone and explain everything. Together they'd worked out a plan of attack. Ivy was to take me home and get me into my comfort clothes while Sasha would go to the store for the emergency supplies of Butter Pecan, Chunky Monkey and Rocky Road.

"Emma? Ice cream therapy doesn't work if you're just staring at the spoon. I bought all this ice cream and you're not even eating it!"

Sasha nudges me with her foot.

"I guess I'm not that hungry." I pull the knitted afghan on my legs higher. Ever since we got home, I've had a chill that I can't seem to shake. I took a hot shower and I'm wearing leggings under my pajamas but I'm still cold inside. It feels like something died in me.

Ivy puts down her spoon. "Let's skip to the guy-bashing segment of the evening. I'll start with how bad Jon's breath smelled in the morning. Then you can go. Tell us how he's secretly half bald and that sexy hair is really a hairpiece. Or maybe how he used to clip his toenails in bed. Or how small his—"

"Whoa! I don't need to know about that. I'm going to have a hard enough time looking him in the eye at Kay and Eli's wedding as it is." Sasha stills before her eyes lift to mine. "Sorry. I'm sure you don't want to hear about that."

"No, it's okay. Somebody should be happy."

Her phone beeps and she pulls it out of her bag. "Speaking of Kay, I have to go. I was supposed to be at her place an hour ago." She pulls me into a hug. "I'll call you tomorrow, okay."

Ivy gets up and walks her to the door. By the back and forth whispers and the covert glances, I can tell they're talking about me. After Sasha's gone, Ivy comes back and sits on the couch right next to me.

"I haven't pushed you to talk about it any more because I figured you needed a break. But you can talk about him if you need to."

This is the thing I've missed the most about us. My sister being my friend. Being able to tell her about what's going on in my life and knowing that she'll have advice and a shoulder to lean on.

"Talking is not going to fix this one. I really screwed up. Getting back into school has been my focus for so long I lost sight of what's right for a minute there. I saw the money as an easy solution to a problem that I had no idea how to deal with. Except the old me would have known that there are no easy solutions."

"It's not your fault. We both kind of fell apart after… that day." Her eyes fill with tears. "I felt so guilty for not being there. Maybe those monsters wouldn't have chosen our house if there was another car in the driveway. Maybe we could have overpowered them somehow if we'd been together. Maybe, Maybe, Maybe."

I grab her hand and she squeezes it tight. We never really talked about that day. At first because it was too fresh and then later because bringing up the past was too painful. I never knew that she'd harbored these thoughts. Maybe we could have helped each other with the feelings of guilt and regret if we'd been able to share them.

"You know it's not your fault, Ivy. It's their fault. The people who did it."

"I know. But the way we feel doesn't always make sense. But I'm starting to think that by keeping this house, we're just keeping the worst part of our lives front and center."

"I've been thinking the same thing. This whole situation with school got me thinking. I got some scholarship offers for schools out of state. If I take those, then I'll be able to finish school and get away from all of this for a while. Get a fresh start."

Ivy sits up abruptly, her ice cream falling out of her hand and leaving milky white droplets on the front of her shirt. “Em, no! I just got you back. Or I guess I should say, I just got my head out of the sand since I was the one who let a guy come between us. I don’t want you to leave.”

She’s sincere and finally seems to understand what her emotional desertion has been like for me this past year.

“It won’t be forever. Just for school. I’ve gotten some offers from schools in North Carolina. Their financial aid packages are really attractive. I wasn’t considering them before because I just couldn’t imagine leaving Virginia. This is home, you know?”

“It is home. That’s why you need to stay here. Do you really think things are over with Tank?”

I close my eyes. I’m already tired of thinking about it. All I’ve done since that conversation in the stairwell is rehash all the ways I screwed up. All the chances I had to tell him what his father was up to. I wanted to protect him from the truth but the truth wasn’t what he needed to fear. My deception hurt him worse than the truth ever could have.

And now it’s too late. It’s almost nine o’clock. Visiting hours are over and he’s probably back at home. But he hasn’t called or texted. He’s not going to come after me.

“He was so angry. And disappointed. I think that was worse. I betrayed him and now he won’t believe that what we had was real. He’ll always think that I was there because of the money.”

Ivy scoots over on the couch and takes the ice cream container out of my hands. She sets it on the coffee table carefully and then pulls me into a hug. We sit there like that until she reaches over and grabs my ice cream.

"I still say Ben and Jerry are our soul mates."

And for the first time in a long time, I have my sister back.

Tank

One week later ...

It's the weirdest thing to be in my brother's house drunk off my ass. I turn my head to the side and watch Finn. He's spinning slightly. Gabe and Zack followed us to Finn's penthouse from the hospital since he lives the closest.

He also has a fully stocked bar.

"Okay, big guy. Let's get you on the couch." Gabe hoists me up from the floor where I've been for the past hour. I think I was on the couch at one point but after a few glasses of scotch, things start to get a little unclear.

"He's just going to end up on the floor again. Trust me, I know this from years of experience dealing with him." Finn rolls his eyes at me.

"I'm going to give him a pass. It's been a rough week. For all of us." Gabe pointed out.

We've been back and forth to the hospital all week, taking turns sitting at our father's bedside. I'm not sure why the others feel obligated to do it but I'm still wrestling with the guilt of putting him there. Through it all, my brothers have been right beside me. Despite their support, there's a gap they can't fill. It's amazing how you can be lonely in a room full of people.

"I'm so glad you guys are all here. Because we're *brothers*." I point at Gabe and then at Zack. Finally I point at Finn. When I lean toward him, I almost topple off the couch.

He slaps my hand away. "Let me see it again."

I know what he wants and he can't have it. Emma is mine. At least, she *was* mine. Until I realized that she was just one more of my father's minions.

When I don't hand it over, Finn leans down and tries to pull it forcibly from my pocket. The full state of my inebriation is apparent when I realize I can't fight him off. He pushes my hands aside easily and yanks the envelope I've been carrying around the past week from my pocket.

"Fuck off, Finn."

He just grins and looks over at Gabe and Zack. "He's a pissy drunk."

They chuckle along with him and my head falls back on the couch behind me. "I'm a sucker. That's what I am."

Finn pulls out the check and holds it up to the light.

Zack peers over his shoulder. "I can't believe she didn't cash it."

Finn puts it back in the envelope. "So she carried a million dollar check in her purse *uncashed* for the better part of twenty-four hours? The average person would have run to the nearest bank. Instead she came home to you. Then she woke up with you. Then she came to the hospital to talk to you."

"I don't need a list. I was there, remember?"

He sits forward and glares at me. "Were you? Really? Because I'm starting to wonder if you're remembering events correctly. Otherwise none of this makes sense."

My head is really starting to hurt. I shouldn't have a hangover before I'm even done drinking. Because I'm not done. Not by a long shot.

"Hell, I'd have been on a plane to Tahiti," Zack comments. After that he takes another swig of his beer and goes back to ignoring us.

"We have to be on g-guard against this kind of thing now." The words are hard to get out. But I need to tell Finn. I need to warn him. "Women will want to get close to us just because we have money."

He doesn't look impressed. "There are women who want to get close to you because you ride a motorcycle. There's no way you can know a woman's motivations but you can judge her actions."

"Her actions…" Suddenly the entire situation is insanely funny to me. I chuckle to myself while Finn just shakes his head. When I finally get my amusement under control, I point at him.

"Her actions are … that … she accepted money to be with me," I finish triumphantly.

"Actually, she was offered money and didn't immediately take it. I didn't hesitate when he offered me money so she's got more willpower than I've got. You still want to be my brother?"

"That sounds like a trick question." Gabe collapses on the couch next to me.

"Whose side are you on?" From this angle I can finally look at him up close and he really does look like me. Like a more handsome version of me.

I wonder if Emma would think he was handsome. He looks more like the kind of guy that she should be with. Clean cut and educated. Not spiked hair, leather and a body full of scars and battle wounds. Maybe my father will pay her to seduce him, too. She's already got Finn wrapped around her little finger.

And me. She's already got me … something.

Gabe seems amused by my staring. "I'm just saying maybe you aren't the only person our dear father manipulated?"

I have the feeling that what he's saying makes sense but I'm so tired. All I want to do is be alone with my anger and my despair. I point at Gabe. "You should get out." Then I point at Finn. "You should get out, too."

"I'm not getting out. This is my place, asshole."

Zack looks over from his perch near the window. "What about me? Should I stay?" He smirks and takes another sip of his beer.

Now they're all staring at me. And laughing at me, too. "I'm too drunk for this."

Then I promptly pass out.

* * * * *

The next morning, I open my eyes slowly, tentatively. The

splitting pain behind my forehead seems to be a warning of what's to come. It's too bright in here and my back hurts. When I turn my head, it feels like my brain is being assaulted by a hundred tiny men with hammers.

"What happened?"

Finn appears in the doorway of the living room. He's already dressed in jeans and a green sweater. "You got shitfaced. That's what happened."

Gabe comes out of the kitchen. "It's alive!"

I grimace as his loud voice brings back the small army of cavemen in my head. "Is it? Because IT feels like roadkill."

Gabe disappears back into the kitchen and then reemerges with a cup of coffee. "Drink this."

The smell coming from the cup is like nirvana. I nurse the coffee while they both watch me. Finally I can't take it anymore. "What?"

"Do you even remember last night?" Finn demands.

"More than I'd like to."

I remember all of Finn's arguments actually and in the light of day they make sense. None of us could say no to the money our father offered. So, was Emma any better or worse than we were? The old man actually seems kind of fond of her. I wonder if he thought he was playing matchmaker in a twisted way.

It would be just the kind of screwed up thing that he would think was normal.

The doorbell rings and Finn answers it. "Mom! What are you doing here?"

I immediately sit up straighter and try to look alive. Even though I'm a grown man, I still don't want my mom to catch me hungover. Mom nods hello to Gabe and Zack as she hangs her coat on the back of one of the bar stools. She met them a few days ago and it wasn't nearly as awkward as we all thought it would be.

"I've been thinking, boys."

Mom sits down on the couch next to me. I blink several times, hoping I don't smell like alcohol.

"After everything that happened, well, I shouldn't be but I was worried about your father. But when I called the hospital to check on him, they wouldn't tell me anything. So, I decided to come over. Are you all getting ready to go visit him?"

Finn glances at me. "We're trying to convince Tank not to let the best thing that ever happened to him walk away because of something our dad started. He still hasn't called Emma."

I scowl at Finn. He was always a tattletale. "I'm not letting her walk away. She walked away on her own. Now I'm just thinking about everything. And she hasn't called me either." I glance over at my mom. She's been strangely quiet on the whole subject. "This whole week, you haven't said much about Emma. That's not like you."

"I don't want to influence you. It's your decision. But I do want to ask you a question."

I don't trust this casual inquiry at all. My mom knows how to get all up in my head and make me face things when I'm being an idiot without ever raising her voice or being pushy.

"Do I have a choice?"

She ignores my smart response. "Why didn't you tell me about your dad being in town when you first found out?"

Now I really am an idiot. I should have known that Finn and I weren't off the hook for that. Even though we had good reason, my mom is definitely going to require a good explanation for why we'd lie to her face.

"I was ashamed, Mom."

"Oh sweetheart. Ashamed of what?"

"Ashamed that I was taking money from him. He hurt you. He hurt us. But I just needed the money to help you. It seemed like the only solution at the time."

She nods thoughtfully. Then she peeks over at me mischievously. "I wonder if that's how Emma felt, too."

Gabe grins and looks between us. "Oh, she's good. Even I didn't see that coming."

Mom smiles. "Thank you. I thought it was artfully done."

I'm amazed and irritated at the same time. "You're being awfully charitable towards her about this. She did accept the job after all. No one forced her to do it."

Mom gives me a knowing look. "Honey, I know exactly how convincing Maxwell Marshall can be. Your Emma didn't stand a chance."

Finn chimes in. "Do you really want to let her go? She thinks you're one in a million, bro. How many guys can say that?"

I pull out the check from my pocket and stroke the now

crumpled envelope. Every moment I've shared with Emma over the past month flies through my head. The peace, the sharing, and the laughter.

The morning after she caught me fighting stands out in my head in particular. *Leaving you is the last thing I ever want to do.* I realize the statement is as true now as it was then.

"I need to call her."

"Go over there. Find her. This is not a complicated covert operation. It's a simple find and rescue," Finn insists.

My mom holds up a hand. "First, let's go to the hospital and visit your father. I want to thank him personally for paying my hospital bill. He didn't have to do that. "

"And after that, we'll go with you," Gabe says. "For moral support."

"Or in case she doesn't forgive you," Zack adds.

Gabe shoots him an exasperated look. "You're not supposed to say that out loud."

I laugh, setting off a new ache in the back of my skull. "You guys don't have to do that."

"That's what brothers do."

I'm surprised to hear the statement come from Gabe. We haven't known each other that long so I wouldn't be surprised if he didn't feel any obligation toward me at all. But the support means a lot. More than I can say.

"Plus, you might need us to help you get drunk again," Zack adds.

Chapter Sixteen

Emma

The corridor outside Mr. Marshall's hospital room is empty. But when I enter the room, two large men stand up, blocking my path. It's the same guys that came into the room that day when we figured out that Jon was stealing from him. They don't seem to remember me though. Or at least they don't move, anyway.

"Hi, I just wanted to see if Mr. Marshall was okay."

"Emma? Is that you? Let her pass, Royce."

The biggest guy moves aside so I can squeeze by. Mr. Marshall is propped up in the bed reading the newspaper and has a cell phone to his ear. He has a pair of glasses perched on the end of his nose. If he wasn't in a hospital gown and strapped to a bunch of machines, I would think he was preparing for a day at the office.

"Mr. Marshall, what are you doing? Aren't you supposed to be resting?"

I glance back at the big guys guarding the door. "Is he allowed to do this stuff?" They look at each other and then back at me and shrug.

Exasperated, I hold out my hand for the phone. "I'm pretty sure this isn't allowed when you've just had a heart attack."

He grins and says something to the person on the other end. Then he hangs up and hands me the phone. "I had my guys sneak in the phone and got one of those cute little nurses to bring me a paper. I have to keep up with what's going on."

I take the paper and fold it up. "I think the world will keep spinning even if you take a few days off."

He grumbles but finally sits back. "I heard about what happened. I wish I'd been there. I didn't know that Jon had hurt you."

I touch the fading bruise on my cheek. Over the past week, it's turned a strange array of colors. Now it looks like a faint purplish splotch. "I wasn't sure what to do. Tank didn't know what was going on then and I didn't want him to find out. I was bound by my own lies."

"It's not often that I say this but I'm sorry. I was only trying to help you but it ended up doing the opposite. I never wanted you to get hurt. I'm surprised Tank didn't kill him when he found out."

"Tank and I ..." I stop, unsure of how to describe the state of things between us. Non-existent is probably the most accurate. He hasn't called me or come by the house at all in the past week. It's like we never knew each other at all.

Mr. Marshall's smile falters. "I'm sorry, Emma."

"It's not your fault. Not really. Because I could have said no."

"No, you couldn't have." He shakes his head sadly. "No one says 'no' to a million dollars. Trust me. I'm in the position to know that for sure."

"I did. I gave the check back to Tank. He came to see you after that and I haven't seen him since."

His mouth falls open slightly. I've never seen him look like this. I giggle at his expression. If I'm truly the first person who has ever turned down one of his deals, then I guess that's why.

"But at least something good came out of all of this. Your sons are speaking to you now. I saw them all here at the hospital that day. That's good news, right?" I clasp his hand gently.

His hand tightens around mine. "Yes, they were here. Except for one. All except for one."

Now this is interesting news. "Oh, you have another son?"

"Yes. Lucas."

He says the name with reverence. I've noticed that his whole demeanor changes when he talks about his children. Even though he wasn't there when they were growing up and basically was the worst father ever, he really does seem to love them. It makes no sense to me but the evidence is undeniable.

He loves his kids. Despite his strange way of contacting them, he actually wants to spend time with them and have them in his life.

"I know your secret now, Mr. Marshall."

His eyes shoot to mine and for the first time, he looks afraid. "What do you mean?"

I pat his hand gently. "That you're a big old softie. Under that stern exterior that everyone else sees, you love your sons."

"That I do." He takes a deep breath and then struggles to sit up a little higher against the pillows. "But wait, what about your schooling? Your dreams to become a veterinarian and help animals? How will you do it now?"

"I've got some scholarship offers to schools in North Carolina. It'll be a chance for me to make a fresh start. I can forget about all the bad things in my past and just move on with my life. That's why I'm here. I wanted to say goodbye."

The idea that I'll be gone soon brings an unexpected well of emotion to the fore. I cough a little to keep myself from tearing up. For a little while, visiting Mr. Marshall made me feel like I had a family again. But I have to deal with reality or I'll never be able to be a part of it.

It's time to move forward.

* * * * *

There's a chorus of voices out in the hallway. The two guards stand but then immediately move back. Tank steps in the room, followed by Finn and his other two brothers. Then someone else steps in behind them. When Finn moves to the side I can see who it is.

Claire.

Shame brings a blush to my cheeks. "I should go. Your family is here to see you. I just wanted to say goodbye."

"Goodbye?" Tank interrupts. "Where are you going?"

He stares at me until I meet his gaze. It's so hard to look at him, knowing how much pain I've caused him. Even though it was the last thing I wanted to do, I hurt him. Now I'm here, making his time with his father uncomfortable.

I shake my head and look back to Mr. Marshall. His eyes are kind, like he understands that I need to get away. "I have to go."

He squeezes my hand. "Go on. I'm going to miss you, Miss Shaw."

I don't look at Tank as I walk out. I have to pass Claire to get to the door. Facing her is even harder than facing the others. They all know what I did but with her, it's worse. It feels like I betrayed her, too.

Right before I reach the door, I pause and look at her. "I'm so sorry. You have no idea how much."

To my surprise, she pulls me into a hug. The tears I've been holding back so far finally overflow. When I pull back, she wipes my cheeks. "You have no idea how much *I understand*." Then she looks over at Mr. Marshall.

I nod at Finn as I pass and then I'm finally in the hall. After the small confines of the room, it feels freeing.

"Wait, Emma." Tank appears in the doorway. It's pathetic but after a week of no contact at all, my eyes eat up the sight of him like visual candy. He's as beautiful as always, even with bags under his eyes and a good bit of stubble on his cheeks. I take my time memorizing his face.

It'll have to last me for the rest of my life.

"Where are you going? Back there, you said ..." He places an arm against the doorjamb. "What was all that about saying goodbye?"

"It's okay, Tank. We don't really have to do this part. This thing with us has been backward from the beginning. Do we really need to break up when we never really got together in the first place?"

He takes my hand and leads me to the waiting room. It's filled with people already. He lets out a disgusted sound and then pulls me to the same stairwell where we argued before.

"I was coming to see you after this."

"You were?" He doesn't look angry but I'm too numb from the past week to know whether that's reality or if I'm just spaced out.

"Yeah, I was. I've spent the past week in and out of this hospital visiting my father and spending time with my brothers. But it always felt like something was missing. *Someone* was missing. You."

My heart starts beating so hard that I need to take a breath to steady myself. "I wanted to be here. But I didn't think you'd want to see me."

Tank grabs my hands. "Here's the thing. I know how I feel

about you. Ever since the beginning, being around you has been one of the only times I feel calm. Happy. You center me, Emma. But I'll always wonder which memories between us are tainted. Were you only with me for the money while cooking dinner for my family? Or were you thinking about the money that night when you cleaned the cut on my arm and I held you all night? Which memories are real and which are manufactured?"

I shake my head. "None of them. From the very beginning, I couldn't do what I was supposed to do. I couldn't see you as a job. You wouldn't let me. You kept surprising me with how smart and funny and sweet you are."

"Sweet, huh?"

Even in the midst of a serious conversation, he can manage to be arrogant. I laugh. "Yeah, I'll admit it this once. You're incredibly sweet. And when I was with you, all the bad stuff went away for a while. I've never been happier than when I was with you."

"That's exactly how I feel. So, I don't care about what my father did or didn't do anymore. I'm in love with you, Emma. And I don't want you going anywhere." His head descends slowly, his eyes on mine the whole time. Then he kisses me and all thoughts, all worries, and all fear dissolves.

It's just his lips on mine and the knowledge that he loves me.

A door opens on one of the floors above us and there's the rhythmic stomp, stomp, stomp, of feet on the stairs.

"I guess we should go back. We're not supposed to be in here." I look up at the open staircase above us.

Tank grins. "I don't care. Break the rules with me, Emma."

I glance back at the open air above us, and then launch myself into his arms. He catches me and I wrap my legs around his waist. As we kiss, someone passes by us going up the staircase and I don't even care to look.

Tank is the only thing I want to see.

"So you had an interesting strategy for getting my attention. I asked you out for weeks in a row and you refused every time. I've never seen that used as a way to get a date but I suppose it worked."

"I wasn't playing hard to get. As hard as this may be on your ego, I said no because I didn't want to go out with the bad boy in leather who looked like nothing but trouble. Besides, that was way before your dad even made the offer."

"It was? Well, when did he make the offer?"

"Um, it was actually the day you showed up at the club. Which was a totally crazy coincidence now that I look back on it."

Tank pulls away, a strange look on his face. "Wait, that can't be right. It must have been before that."

"No, it was that day. I remember so clearly because it was the strangest day ever. I got offered a million dollars in the afternoon, then my crappy car wouldn't start and then I got fired from my strip club waitressing job. Strangest day ever."

Tank chuckles and then it turns into a full belly laugh. He picks me up and spins us around.

"What? What is going on?"

"There was no 'job'. My father was matchmaking, Emma. I

remember that day clearly, too. I was just leaving my brother's place when my boss called asking me for a favor. I'd just been telling Finn that I'd signed the papers accepting my father's terms."

"Wait, what? That doesn't make sense. So that day when Mr. Marshall offered me the money—"

"I had already signed," Tank finished. "There was no need for you to convince me to do anything because my father had already gotten what he wanted. Except apparently that wasn't the *only* thing he wanted. He wanted to give you the money because he likes you. This was the only way he could figure out how to do it. And it was his way of pushing us together."

Joyous laughter bubbles up inside me. "I knew it. He's just a big ole' softie."

Tank leans against the wall, pulling me into the cradle of his thighs. "I don't know what the future will bring but I need to know that you'll be a part of it. I *need* to know that you'll be with me as I face it."

I cup his face and pull him down so he can see the truth in my eyes. "That's exactly what I want, too. I was so scared that you wouldn't want to see me anymore."

His lips brush across my forehead. "My brother pointed out something that I couldn't ignore this morning. You turned down a million dollars for me. If that doesn't prove that you're really in this for me, then I don't know what ever could." He kisses me again and we collapse back against the wall, entwined in each other's arms.

"I guess since that million dollars isn't dirty money, maybe I shouldn't have given it back to you then, huh?"

Tank grins at me and then pulls something from his back pocket. It's the envelope I gave him but it's all crumpled and creased.

"You've been carrying that around this whole time?"

He shrugs and his arms tighten around my middle. "It was my last connection to you. But you can have it back. I honestly don't care."

I shake my head. "I've already got exactly what I want right here. And it has nothing to do with money."

Everything is still up in the air. I'm not sure where I'm going to live, where I'm going to go to school or how I'm going to pay for any of it. I know that I don't want Tank paying for it but beyond that I haven't got a clue. But I know that I can figure it out.

And that Tank will be with me through it all.

Epilogue

Tank

One month later . . .

I enter Finn's penthouse balancing two large pizzas under one arm and carrying a six-pack of beer in the other. I look over my shoulder at Eli, who stands uncertainly behind me.

"Come on in. Have a beer. Take a load off."

He waves at Finn, Gabe and Zack who are sitting on the couch. There's already a basketball game playing on the big screen.

"Guys, this is my boss, Elliott Alexander. Eli, my brothers. Finn is in the armchair, the one who looks like my clone is Gabe and the one with the Mohawk is Zack."

Eli waves amidst the chorus of hellos. "You guys look like you're set. I won't stay. I just wanted to bring you that information you asked for, Tank."

I set the beer down on the floor and hand the pizzas off to Gabe. I take the envelope he's holding out. He seems uncomfortable and I can't get why. We've never really hung out before but I wanted him to meet my brothers. Yet, he's acting like he can't wait to get out of here.

"Okay, if you can't stay I understand. I just figured you might want to escape for a while."

He drops his head. "Yeah. I just bought the house and it's been taken over by a bunch of women I haven't seen since I was in Sunday school as a kid."

"Eli just got engaged," I mention to the others. "His fiancée is in the middle of planning the wedding."

Zack gets up and walks to the kitchen. When he comes back, he hands a beer to Eli. "You probably need this."

Eli laughs but stops when he sees me ripping open the envelope. "Hey, I'm going to give you guys some privacy for a minute." He doesn't look at me before walking into the kitchen.

Zack looks at me and shrugs. "What's going on with him?"

"I have no idea—" I stop in mid-sentence when I pull out the stack of files in the envelope. I asked Eli to assist with a background check that was proving more challenging than I'd expected. He's got a magic touch with finding things that other people want to keep hidden.

My brother Lucas obviously didn't want to be found.

Zack follows me as I walk over to the couch still scrutinizing the pictures. Gabe and Finn look up as I step in front of the television.

"I think my boss is trying to distance himself just in case any of you turn out to be closet racists." They all look over at Eli, who is currently bent over trying to pretend he's fascinated by the contents of Finn's refrigerator.

I look too, trying to see him through their eyes. He's a heavily muscled, dark-skinned guy with a shaved head. I've never thought too much about what he looks like before, mainly because it doesn't matter. He's an exceptional boss and an even better friend. That's all I care about. And without even asking, I know my brothers are the same way.

I raise my voice. "Eli, you can come over here now. It's cool."

He looks up at the sound of my voice. "You sure?" He glances over at the others, uncertainly. At their nods of agreement, he walks over and perches on the arm of the couch.

I turn to the others. "I needed Eli's special touch to find someone. He came through, as usual."

I hold up one of the pictures. A tall, thin young man with light brown skin and curly hair is shown crossing the street. He's wearing sunglasses but there's no denying that he looks like us.

"That's him?" Gabe reaches out to take the picture. When he's done looking at it, he passes it to Zack.

"Yeah. Lucas Brown Marshall. Age 22. Also known as Luke," I say, reading from the typed summary sheet that Eli included. "He's some kind of child prodigy. He graduated high school at 16 and college at 19. He owns a software development company. It says here that when he was on summer vacation one year, he created the program that the majority of the state's hospitals use to keep patient's digital records secure."

"I guess he was bored that summer," Gabe comments.

Finn claps him on the back and snorts out a laugh. "Yeah, I guess so."

I continue reading. "His mother, Anita Brown Marshall, owns a bakery called *Anita's Place*."

Gabe sits forward. "I've been there a bunch of times. Best damn cheesecake I've ever had. So, what's the plan? Should we go there and wait for him to show up?"

I look at some of the other pictures. Eli retreated because he was worried that my brothers' initial reactions would be less than positive. But what if Luke's reaction isn't positive? It makes sense that he was so hard to find now that I know he's some kind of cyber genius. He's probably been taking steps to erase his digital footprint since he started using a computer. And if he's taking that many precautions, he might not take too kindly to being found.

For any reason.

"I'm not so sure about that. A gang of white guys rolls up and says '*Surprise, we're your brothers*' ?"

Zack makes a face. "Right. Because I can't see anything going wrong with that plan."

There's a beat of silence and then we all laugh. Finn has the picture now. He hands it back to me and I slide it back in the envelope.

"Look, I want to say something." They all quiet down and I try to get my thoughts together. "The past few months have been insane. My mom was diagnosed with cancer again and the father I haven't seen in years is suddenly not only in my life but making some pretty crazy demands."

The others nod at that.

"We still don't know what old Max is up to or what any of this ultimately means but we have a choice going forward. We can let him call all the shots or we can stick together and figure this thing out. I'm counting on us being stronger as a group than apart. And no matter what else happens, I'm happy I got some more brothers out of the deal."

Finn raises his beer in agreement. The others follow suit. "To brothers."

Eli raises his beer, too. "Now, you know that's something I can drink to. To brothers."

Finn stands and then knocks me out of the way of the television. "Now that the speeches are over, get the hell out of the way so I can see who's winning!"

I punch him in the arm and then lean on the edge of his chair, observing him and the others as they scream at the screen.

There's a certain peace in surrounding yourself with people that you trust. And I'm finally at peace. I know that after we're done kicking it, that I'll be going home to a woman who loves me and who'll stand by me through anything.

And I know that no matter what Maxwell Marshall has in store for us in the future, that I'll have my brothers behind me the whole way.

Because that's what brothers do.

The End

You just finished reading the first book in the Blue-Collar Billionaires series. TANK is a spinoff from the *USA TODAY* Bestselling ALEXANDERS series so stay tuned for a special excerpt of Eli's book, *All I Need is You*.

All I Need is You **(Eli + Kay)**

is available now!

When the man she loves leaves town after their steamy kiss, Kaylee Wilhelm is done. She has no time for pining after her former bodyguard.

But when she's targeted by a stalker, Eli is the only one who can protect her. And Eli is willing to do whatever it takes to protect the one woman who gets under his skin.

Anything except fall in love…

EXCERPT of *All I Need is You*

KAYLEE SHOVED THE books on her night table in the drawer. Her eyes swept over the rest of the room frantically. Hopefully she hadn't left anything embarrassing lying around. She wasn't used to having guys at her apartment. Especially not men like Elliott.

Big, masculine men that she fantasized about every night.

The hair on the back of her neck stood up and she didn't have to look to know that he was standing in the doorway. Her apartment wasn't that big, but it suddenly seemed exponentially smaller with Eli sucking up all her oxygen.

"Tank finished his assessment before we got here. We're all clear." Eli stepped in and looked around. "Where do you normally keep the figurine?"

Kay pointed to the top of her dresser. Eli walked over and looked down at her collection. He touched one and the sight of his thick fingers stroking the delicate china shouldn't have seemed erotic at all. But the image of this big, strong man handling tiny breakables with such care struck her as incredibly tender. Would that be how he treated a woman in bed? Like she was delicate, precious?

Or would he push her hard, demand things she didn't know how to give? Warmth spread to her face just thinking about it.

Not that you'll ever find out.

"There's an empty space here. He didn't even bother to push the others closer together to conceal what he took."

Kay hated to even think of it. Someone had been in her

apartment, touching her things. Had he been here while she was home alone? While she was with her daughter?

While they were sleeping?

She shivered and grabbed the duffel bag she kept underneath her bed. Her favorite nightshirt was on top of the comforter, so she shoved that in the bag. Then she pulled open the drawers in her nightstand and added a big handful of underwear and bras. She didn't even look at how much she was taking, just grabbed blindly. Who cared, really, what she wore? All she cared about was getting out of here. Would she ever be able to relax in this room again without wondering if someone was watching?

She crossed to the dresser where Eli stood and yanked open the last drawer. In went several pairs of jeans, then she yanked open another drawer and added a big armful of sweaters.

"Kay, what are you doing?"

"Packing. I just want to get out of here."

She struggled with the zipper on the bag, almost breaking a nail on the metal teeth. Her breath came in harsh pants until little black spots danced in front of her eyes.

"Kay, calm down. Just hold on."

She struggled against his hold, but he held her securely in his grip, her back to his front. His arms wrapped around her, keeping her from moving but not holding her so tight as to cause pain. Eventually Kay stopped fighting and allowed her head to fall back against Eli's chest.

"Hey, hey. It's all right. Just calm down." He rubbed her arms gently, soothing her.

Kay finally stopped wrestling with him and allowed him to hold her. She closed her eyes and took a deep breath. It was a foolish moment of weakness, but for just a second, she soaked up the comfort and warmth of being in his arms.

"We're safe here. You've got a great security system. I already had Tank check it out and it hasn't been tampered with. I don't know how this guy got your figurine, but he didn't break in to do it."

Tears welled up, but she squeezed her eyes closed, swallowing back the sudden flood of emotion. There was no time for nonsense or feeling sorry for herself.

"Why would someone do this, Eli?"

"I don't know, angel." He spoke in a hush, the words flowing over her in a soft puff of breath.

His features tightened, and for the second time in recent memory, she allowed herself to soak up the masculine presence that was Elliott Alexander: the smooth dark skin, the high cheekbones, the long straight blade of his nose, and the sinfully full lips. It was a harsh face, not quite as elegantly hewn as his brothers' faces, but one that she vastly preferred. It looked like safety.

It looked like strength.

"I'm okay now. I promise I won't freak out on you again." She stood reluctantly. As wonderful as it felt to be held in his arms, there was only so much she could take before she lost all sense of propriety and threw herself at him again. She already knew he wasn't interested. When you kissed a guy and he responded by leaving town, that was plenty clear enough.

"It's okay to be freaked out, Kay. As long as you know that I won't let anything happen to you."

Kay nodded and dropped the duffel bag on her bed. She didn't have enough room to put him up in style, but at the very least she could rustle up some extra pillows and a blanket for him.

"I'm sorry I don't have a guest room. Or an air mattress."

Eli gave her one of his trademark *are you kidding* looks. "I'm not supposed to be on vacation, Kay. The couch is fine. Now, what about Hope?"

Kay gasped. Shame flooded her face. She'd told her mom that she'd pick up Hope by eight o'clock and she was already twenty minutes late. She pulled out her cell phone and hit the first speed dial.

Eli walked away to give her some privacy. Luckily, her father answered, so she was able to explain things with a minimum of fuss. As expected, her parents were thrilled to keep Hope overnight.

When she turned, Eli was watching her with an inscrutable expression. Unsure what to make of his sudden change in demeanor, Kay pushed past him and pulled open the door to the linen closet in the hallway. Several towels fell out and hit her in the face.

"Don't worry about that now." Eli took the towels from her arms and shoved them in the closet. "We need to talk first."

"About what?"

"Everything. Clearly I missed something when I was digging into your life last year. It's time to rectify that."

"But nothing has changed. I don't do anything interesting. So what's there to talk about?"

Eli stopped and nailed her with an intense look. "I need to know who you've been with since last summer." He moved closer and Kay inhaled, immediately assaulted by his unique scent—warm and rich and disarming. She looked up at him, her senses swirling from the intoxicating blend of reactions that only Eli could cause.

"We need to talk about your lovers."

** *All I Need is You* is available now!

ABOUT THE AUTHOR

New York Times & USA TODAY Bestselling author M. Malone lives in the Washington, D.C. metro area with her three favorite guys: her husband and their two sons. She likes dramatic opera music, staid old men wearing suspenders, claw-foot bathtubs, and unexpected surprises.

The thing she likes best is getting to make up stuff for a living.

www.MMaloneBooks.com